Bull City Blues

Wynton Sellers

Published in Clermont, FL
Cover Designs: Design for Writers
Edits: Before You Publish - Book Press

Published and printed in the United States of America

ISBN: 979-8-9932349-1-5

Sellers, Wynton

Bull City Blues – First edition

www.wyntonsellers.com

Chapter One

Jabari Miller huddled in his sleeping bag as a storm raged outside his tent. Thunder shook the ground and lightning crawled across the sky. Strong winds rattled the walls of his tent, and he prayed it would hold. It did not. The tent collapsed on top of him. He reached for the corners of the plastic tarp and wrapped it around his sleeping bag, hoping to at least keep dry. He pulled his knees up toward his chest and lay underneath the layers of fabric, feeling the force of the rain pounding on top of him.

When the worst of the storm had passed, Jabari unzipped his sleeping bag and pulled back the tarp. He crawled out into the darkness and looked around as rain fell steadily upon him. He shined his flashlight around the exterior of the collapsed tent until he found the reason for its failure. The force of the wind had pulled one of the stakes out of the wet ground, so he pulled the tent upright, stretched the guy line outward, and pounded the stake back into the ground. He climbed back into the tent, removed his wet clothing and hung them from a retractable clothesline. Once it was back standing, he pulled on a pair of boxer briefs and slid back into the comfort of his sleeping bag. Lying on his back, he listened to the soothing sound of the rain landing on his re-erected tent and rolling off the sides onto the ground. He closed his eyes and slept.

It was mid-morning when the rain stopped falling. The storm had kept Jabari awake for most of the night, causing him to sleep longer than he had wanted. He looked at his watch and groaned. *I should have been back on the trail hours ago,* he thought. Jabari dressed in a pair of shorts and a tank top and tied the laces of his Merrell hiking shoes. He squeezed a bit of sunscreen into his hand and rubbed it onto his chestnut skin. He packed up his equipment, grabbed his trekking poles, and hit the trail. He would have to hurry to reach the Oak Tree Inn before nightfall.

Jabari moved quickly along the Appalachian Trail, traversing over downed trees and rocky terrain. The trail eventually leveled off into a more manageable path, snaking through the forest and climbing higher into the North Carolina Blue Ridge Mountains. He settled into a steady pace, placing one foot in front of the other and remaining mindful of the energy he exerted along the way.

Seeing a road ahead, Jabari pulled a map from the side of his bag and looked it over as he tramped. He calculated the distance to his destination and quickened his pace. As he came to the road, he saw a woman sitting on the hood of a blue Honda Accord, staring down at her phone. She wore a pair of black leggings and a red tank top. Car grease stained her face, and her braided hair was formed in a hasty ponytail.

"No. No," the woman said, and slammed the phone down beside her. She let out a deep breath, looked up at the sun, and wiped the sweat from her face with the palm of her hand.

Jabari stepped out of the forest and proceeded on toward the road with the sound of dried leaves and twigs crushing and cracking underfoot. The woman turned to him and leaped down onto the ground and ran around to the driver's-side door of her car.

"Whoa." Jabari raised both hands, dropping his trekking poles. "Calm down, lady. I don't want any trouble."

"Where did you come from?" she asked.

Jabari pointed to the forest. "From there."

"What do you mean, from there?" she asked.

Jabari pointed at the forest again. "The Trail."

The woman looked again at the thicket of trees, and as her eyes settled on the Appalachian Trail, which was covered in debris from the storm, her mouth fell agape in amazement. She fixed her eyes on the trekking poles lying on the ground near Jabari's feet. She placed her hand over her heart and exhaled. "Oh, my gosh. You scared the shit out of me."

"Sorry," Jabari said, with both hands still raised. He kneeled and picked up the poles. "I'll just be on my way," he said, as he crossed the road.

"Do you have a phone?" she asked, calling out.

Jabari turned to face her. "Yes, but it died yesterday."

"What are you doing for communication?"

"I prefer to be off the grid this weekend," he said.

"Damn it." She wiped her brow and placed a hand on her hip. Her caramel skin glistened in the sunlight.

"Are you okay?" he asked.

"No, my car has broken down. You're the first person I've seen, and none of the cars would stop," she said.

"People in these parts stick to themselves," he said.

She leaned back against her car.

Jabari noticed she was wearing one flip-flop, and her other foot was bare. He came back across the road to where she had leaped from the hood of her car and picked up her other shoe. "Is this yours?" When she nodded, he handed it to her.

She looked as if she hadn't noticed that it was gone. "Would you like me to take a look?" Jabari asked.

"Yes, please."

"Pop the hood." He placed his trekking poles and backpack on the ground. "Tell me what happened."

"I was driving along, and the car just stalled and died."

"Just died? No warning?"

"No, everything just shut down, as if someone had flipped a switch," she said.

"Hmm," Jabari murmured, thoughtfully. "How much gas do you have?"

"A half of tank," she said.

"Any smoke or steam?"

"No, nothing like that. It made sort of a dry electric sound," she said.

He lifted the hood and looked over the engine. First, he checked the spark plugs and made sure they were secure. Next, he looked at her vacuum lines, fuel injectors, and liquids. "What did it sound like when you tried to start it?"

"It wouldn't turn over," she said.

"Try it again," he said.

She sat behind the steering wheel and turned the key in the ignition.

He heard the accelerated pace of the spinning engine, which was a sign of little compression and damaged valves. "Whoa, stop," he said.

"What is it?"

"I'm not sure yet." He disconnected the negative battery cable and used a notch on his knife to loosen the screws on the engine cover. "I was afraid of that," he said.

"Afraid of what?"

"It's your timing belt. It's broken."

"Can you fix it?"

"No, I can't," he said, and noticed the disappointment on her face. "Well, I could if I had the proper tools, and a new timing belt. But I don't, and we're sort of in the middle of nowhere, and you may have engine damage, too." He watched her bite her quivering lower lip, as though she wanted to cry.

"What do I do?" she asked.

Jabari sighed. "The nearest town is about fifteen miles away, but it is only eight miles through the forest." He gestured toward the trail. "And I kind of need to get going if I'm going to make it there by sundown."

"Is that where you live?" she asked.

"No, I'm staying at a bed-and-breakfast for the night, and I'll hit the trail again first thing in the morning." He paused. "You're welcome to come with me. We could send a tow truck for your car once we get there."

She looked uncertain and almost frightened by the thought.

"I think I should stay with my car," she said.

Jabari eyed his watch. "Look, I could wait here with you, but if the locals wouldn't stop for you when you were alone, they are certainly not going to stop if I'm here."

"Point taken." She nodded.

"So again, you could either come with me, and I will help you get your car fixed once we get to town, or you could stay here and take your chances. Either way, I need to get going," he insisted.

He watched her eye her car and sigh, as she proceeded to examine his face, and he could see the wheels turning in her head. He was sure that hiking into the forest with a strange man went against every safety precaution her parents had ever taught her. He also understood many found his six-foot-three-inch, muscular frame intimidating. Seeing her distress, Jabari reached into his pocket and retrieved his wallet and revealed a shiny brass badge. "If this makes you feel any better..."

"You're a cop?"

"Durham PD." He grinned and his eyes crinkled with kindness.

"Why didn't you say so?" she said.

"I thought my smile would be disarming enough," he said.

She parted her lips, revealing a set of perfectly aligned teeth.

Jabari looked at her feet, and he worried about her flip-flops. He couldn't imagine she'd make it eight miles through the forest wearing those.

She followed Jabari's gaze down to her feet. "Oh, don't worry." She trotted over to the trunk of her car and pulled out a pair of white socks and muddy tennis shoes. She put them on, tucked a small bifold wallet in the side of her pants and grabbed three bottles of water. "Thirsty?"

"Sure."

She handed Jabari a bottle of water and held the other two. "Let's go."

"Are your doors locked?"

"Yep, but let's make sure," she said. She pressed a button on her key and the car beeped. "There," she said.

"I could hold those for you since your pants are lacking pockets."

She handed him her phone and charger, her keys and her extra bottle of water and watched him place them in a side pocket on his backpack and they were off.

"My name is Simone, by the way," she said, and held out her hand.

"I'm Jabari. It's nice to meet you." He gently grasped her hand and smiled. Her hand was soft and smooth, but her handshake was firm and confident. "So, were you up here burying evidence?" He pointed at her muddy shoes.

"No, officer," she said, and rolled her eyes playfully. "I competed in a mud run yesterday. Have you ever done one?"

"Yes, I have. They're very addictive," he said.

"I know. It was my third," she said.

Jabari was impressed. "Where's your team?"

"They left last night. I was too wiped out to drive, so I got a room and slept straight through the night," she said.

"How many miles did you run?"

"Nine and a half," Simone said.

"I did the Black Ops Run last spring," Jabari said.

"How far was it?" Simone asked.

"Nineteen miles of hell."

They trekked along the narrow path with trees towering above them. Simone's eyes fell on a small creek, where wild Mayapple plants grew along the banks. She pointed to a small chipmunk having a drink. "Look."

Jabari stopped for a closer look, standing silently with Simone for a moment before continuing.

"This is beautiful," Simone said.

"Yes, I love it up here." Jabari beamed with pleasure. "I'd like to do the whole trail one day."

"All the way to Maine?"

"Yes, one day. My dad and I used to hike a section of the trail every summer. He passed away a few years ago, and..."

When his sentence trailed off into silence, Simone placed her hand on his arm. "I'm sorry," she said.

Jabari swallowed hard. "Yeah, it was sort of our special thing."

Simone sighed. "I fantasized about making this trek one day myself. I just didn't know it would be today."

Jabari chuckled. "That's why you must always be prepared." Jabari held up the Boy Scouts' three-finger salute.

Simone followed suit. "And do a good turn daily." She snickered.

Jabari noticed the position of the sun, and it was too low for his liking. He checked his watch and frowned. "We had better get a move on, or we're not going to make it before sundown."

"How much farther?" she asked.

"At least another six miles, and we should have crossed the gorge already." Jabari pulled a rag from his bag and wiped the sweat from his warm, chestnut-colored face.

"We're just strolling along like we don't have a care in the world," she grinned.

Jabari tittered and shook his head.

They moved hastily for about a mile when they came upon the gorge.

Simone gazed down at the clear river running beneath. "Look at those beautiful trees." She pointed to the variety of trees aligning the riverbanks.

Jabari gazed at the large oak, maple, birch, and pine trees. The trees were large and well established, seeming as old as the river running between them.

"Damn it," Jabari exclaimed.

"What's wrong?" she asked.

Jabari pointed to a sign and read it, "Bridge closed, detour three-point-five miles." Jabari looked at his map and saw the difficulty rating of the trail's detour was level 4. He closed his eyes and rubbed the back of his neck.

Chapter Two

Simone looked over the map and shrugged. "We'd better get moving."

The alternate trail traveled alongside the river where the ground was still muddy from the storm. They traversed over downed trees and large slippery rocks.

"Why did I agree to this?" Simone mumbled.

"What's that?" Jabari asked, as he concentrated on every step, leading the way.

"Oh, nothing," she said. "I'm just regretting this decision is all."

The Trail eventually ended near the river's bank. "This is where we cross," Jabari announced.

"How are we supposed to do that?"

"By getting wet." Jabari surveyed the area.

"No way, I'm not doing it." Simone backed up, watching the rushing water.

"We could go back if you want, but now it's getting dark," Jabari said.

Simone looked back in the direction from which they came, and then turned back and gazed at the river again. "Have you done this before?"

"I have," Jabari said.

"Do you think it's safe?"

"It seems to be shallower in this area, and I don't see any signs of underwater hazards, so I think we can cross safely," he said.

Simone placed her hands on her hips and bit her lower lip.

"It's your call," Jabari said.

"Okay, let's go for it."

"Okay, listen. When we cross, face upstream toward the flowing water. Lean forward slightly and try to keep your feet shoulder-width apart and bend your knees to lower your center of gravity. Okay?"

"Got it."

Jabari picked up a stick and tossed it in, watching to see how quickly it moved down river. "Rule of thumb: if the stick moves faster than you can walk, don't cross," he said.

Simone nodded and squinted her eyes.

"I think we're good," he said. He loosened the strap on his backpack. "Are you ready?"

"As ready as I'll ever be," she said.

He handed her one of his trekking poles and wrapped his arm around her waist as she wrapped her arm around his. Jabari used his trekking pole to test the depth of the water before each step.

Halfway across, Simone tightened her grip around Jabari's waist as the cold water covered her thighs.

"Are you okay?"

"I'm fine," she said.

"We're almost there. You're doing good," he said.

Simone followed Jabari's lead. "Lord Jesus, please get us across safely," she murmured.

Once they made it across, Simone sat on a patch of grass shivering in her wet clothes.

Jabari sat beside her and watched the sun dipping below the trees. Light was quickly fading, which would make for a difficult hike into town.

"Thank you, Jabari. I couldn't have done that by myself," she said.

"You're welcome." He winked, and then looked over her caramel face, high cheekbones, and full lips. She met his gaze just before he looked away. "I think we should make camp here tonight. I'll get a fire going and get us warmed up while we dry off."

Jabari removed the tent from his bag. The sun was quickly dropping below the tree line, and he knew he didn't have long to set up camp. Within fifteen minutes, he had pitched his small tent and gathered a hand full of dried pine needles and small twigs. He used the twigs to build an A-frame and placed a handful of pine needles underneath it. He made several piles of larger twigs and sticks, and he gathered another handful of dried grass and pine needles into the bird's nest.

He used his knife to scrape small pieces of flint into the center of the nest, and then he scraped his knife hard against the flint, sending sparks into the center of the nest. When the nest caught fire, Jabari blew air into the center of the flames and placed it underneath the A-frame. When the flames grew, he added larger pieces of wood, until a warm fire illuminated the area.

"Impressive," she said.

Jabari gave a small nod and smile.

The sun was now below the tree line, and its reflection on

the lower clouds created an orange spectacle, making the trees appear to glow.

"Are you hungry?" Jabari asked.

"Yes, I am," she said.

Jabari reached into his bag for more supplies. "There's some trail mix, a banana, and a power bar here," Jabari said.

"That will do," Simone said.

He snapped the banana in half and handed her a piece.

"Thanks," she said, taking a bite.

They shared the trail mix, and finally he handed her the power bar. "You can have it," he said.

Simone ripped it open and bit into it. "Do you have one?"

"No, but I'm fine," he said.

"Here, take the rest of it. You need to eat," she said.

"No. You can finish it."

"What? Do you think I have cooties?" She grinned.

He took it from her and stuffed it into his mouth.

They stared into the fire for a moment before Simone broke the silence, "So, what were the chances I'd break down where I did, and you would come along at just the right moment?"

"Good luck?" Jabari asked.

"No. Good luck would be not breaking down in the first place, but I'll take whatever good fortunes I can get."

"This trip was sort of a last-minute decision for me. Otherwise, I wouldn't even be here," Jabari said.

"What made you decide to come?"

"I'm on leave and thought I'd make the most of my time off."

"Not administrative leave, I hope," she teased.

Jabari frowned and looked away.

"Oh, I'm sorry," she said.

"It's okay."

"What happened?"

"I'd rather not talk about it," he said.

"Understood." Simone leaned back against the log and crossed her legs.

The light from the fire accentuated her curves. Jabari noticed her toned legs and arms and conjectured she spent a lot of time in the gym.

"What do *you* do for a living?" Jabari asked.

"I teach economics at North Carolina Central University."

"Impressive." He pressed his lips and nodded. "Where did you go to school?

"Undergrad at Spellman, and I received my doctorate from Columbia," she answered.

"How long have you been at Central?"

"Only a year. I taught at Columbia before that."

"How did you end up at Central?"

"After graduation, I was offered a position to stay on at Columbia. A great opportunity, but I found the city could be a very lonely place. I didn't have any family there, so it was hard."

"I imagine so."

"I eventually started looking for opportunities to come back home, and finally, a year ago, I received an offer from NCCU. The salary is considerably less, but due to the cost of living in North Carolina, I thought I could manage it," she said.

Jabari leaned back on his side and propped himself up on his elbow. "Are you from Durham?"

"No, Wilmington," she replied.

"Well, Wilmington isn't far at all," Jabari said, and watched as Simone's cheeks dimpled and the flames sparkled in her eyes.

"Do you enjoy your job?" she asked.

"I couldn't imagine doing anything else. Fortunately, my beat includes the neighborhood where I grew up, so I know most of the residents. Some I've known all my life," he said.

"Do you still live there?"

"No, not anymore. The neighborhood has changed since I was a kid," he said, woefully.

"That's unfortunate."

"Yeah," he said, gazing into the flames.

"How long have you been on the force?"

"Five years. I did three years in the Army before going to school for criminal justice. After school, I joined the force."

"I *thought* you were a military man," Simone said.

"What gave it away?"

"You have the air of an officer and a gentleman about you," she said.

"Lou Gossett Jr. or Richard Gere?" Jabari asked.

Simone giggled and took a swig of water. She exhaled and turned back to Jabari. "Do you feel like you're making a difference as a police officer?"

"Sometimes I do, but it seems like I'm always locking up the same people for the same shit," Jabari said.

Simone held up a bottle of water. "Here's to doing what matters," she said, and offered a toast.

Jabari followed suit.

After a moment of silence, she broke it and asked, "Did you serve overseas?"

"In Afghanistan."

"What was it like?"

Jabari sat up and pulled his knees to his chest. "It was the worst year of my life. We were stationed in this little outpost in the Korangal Valley, where we were fired on from every direction—every day, nonstop, without fail. I thought for certain I would die there." Jabari gazed at the fire as flashes of war filled his mind.

Simone sat listening.

"When I came home, I didn't know what to do with myself.

I couldn't sleep without medication, and when I did sleep, the nightmares were so bad, I preferred the insomnia. I was floundering for a while before enrolling in school and earning my degree. I later applied to the Durham Police Department and started my career."

"I'm sorry that happened to you," she said.

"It was war. A lot worse happened to better men than me."

The moon was 90 percent full and its light shined brilliantly along the swiftly flowing waters, shimmering in both directions. They sat quietly for a while, and soon Simone closed her eyes and dozed off.

"You can have the tent. I'll be fine out here," Jabari said.

"Nonsense. It's big enough for the both of us," she said, yawning.

"Not by much," Jabari said.

"Come on, it's getting cold out here." Simone climbed into the tent.

Jabari climbed in next to her and lay down on his back.

As they drifted off to sleep, coyotes howled in the distance.

"Just some coyotes. They're miles away," Jabari said, when he felt Simone stiffen.

Simone turned onto her side facing him. "Thank you for everything. I would hate to be stranded out here alone."

"We'll get you situated in the morning," Jabari said.

She turned over and he felt her snuggle her back up close to his body. He wrapped his arm around her and soon, they both drifted off to sleep.

As Jabari slept, the events that had driven him up into the mountains replayed in his mind. He saw Miles Goodwin's wild eyes. His bloodstained shirt. The knife in his hand. *"Drop the knife,"* Jabari ordered. Gunshots rang in his ears as bullets ripped into Miles Goodwin's chest. Jabari awoke in a cold sweat. He stepped outside of the tent, rekindled the campfire, and located several earthworms. He retrieved his portable fishing rod and pushed a worm onto a fishing hook. Standing on the riverbank, he cast his bait into the river, sat on the cold, hard ground and waited.

Watching the sun ascend beyond the forest, Jabari thought of his troubles, and of Miles Goodwin's lifeless eyes—a vision he couldn't erase. He thought of Simone's reaction when he mentioned he was on leave. He was reminded of her words "Not administrative leave, I hope." And when he didn't answer, he recalled the curiosity in her eyes. *Being from Durham, she would have to know about the shooting. Has she seen the bodycam video?* He wondered.

The tugging on his line brought him back from deep contemplation. He jerked his fishing rod to set the hook and felt a fish fighting to free itself. Jabari slowly reeled it in. He sensed the fish's anger and determination to live on in those waters. He sensed the fish's will to live freely and multiply, but the fish would soon grow tired and face the inevitable. When Jabari pulled their breakfast from the river, its size disappointed him. The poor fish was not big enough to feed two hungry adults. He set the fish aside, baited another hook, and tossed it back into the flowing waters. He soon pulled more impressive fish from the water and immediately descaled and cleaned them the best he could. He found two forked sticks and pushed them into the ground on both sides of the smoldering flames. After soaking two sticks in the river, he placed them into the bellies of the fish and laid them across the fire.

After checking on Simone and finding her still fast asleep, he sat on a log and monitored the roasting of their morning meal. The forest was now fully awake, and like Jabari, the wildlife was hunting for their own nourishment. He closed his eyes and listened to the birds singing and greeting one another. A woodpecker was pecking somewhere in the distance. Upstream, he saw a family of deer grazing along the riverbanks. This was the sort of thing he had escaped to the forest to see—a place he could enjoy solitude with the natural world.

* * *

Simone awoke to the sounds of morning in the forest and noticed Jabari wasn't there. She lay on her back, listening to the river, the singing birds and chirping cicadas. She thought of her car and wondered how much the repairs would cost her. She thought about the trek through the forest and crossing the river. She looked around the small tent and shook her head in disbelief. *I swear, if it wasn't for bad luck, I wouldn't have any at all,* she thought. She rolled onto her stomach and peered out at the man who had offered to help her. She watched him sitting on a log near the fire and gazing into the river, seeming to be in deep contemplation.

She observed his frame, admiring his full pectoral muscles, large biceps and muscular legs. *Handsome man,* she thought. She was reminded of his reaction when she teased him about administrative leave. She thought about the police shooting of the unarmed teenager back home. The shooting had dominated the news in Durham for several months, and the recent release of body-cam footage had sparked protests throughout the city. She consciously decided against watching the video to protect herself from the vicarious trauma that could arise from it. She wondered if Jabari was involved, and if that was the reason he had escaped to the Appalachian Trail. *And what of his dead cell phone? Why does he prefer to be off the grid?* she wondered. She decided to google his name and see what she could find out. She looked around for her phone, before remembering it was dead and in Jabari's bag. *Shit, she murmured.* She knew the police officer who had killed Miles

Goodwin was a white man. *Officer Smith*, she recalled. And with that, she felt relieved.

Simone sat up and pulled her knees to her chest. She gazed at Jabari curiously, before pushing the thoughts of the shooting out of her mind. From the sitting position, she could see two fish roasting over the open flames, and a joyous twinkle lit up her eyes as her lips turned upward, creating a delightful smile.

Chapter Three

As Jabari sat watching the fish roasting over the flames, he heard Simone rustling inside the tent. He turned and saw her climbing out, making her way over to where he was sitting on a log near the flames.

She sat beside him and stretched her arms. "Good morning."

"Good morning, Simone. Are you hungry?"

"I'm starving."

"I thought we should have a hot breakfast," he said.

"It's certainly a step up from last night," she said, sitting beside him, and brushing away some dirt on her leggings and tank top.

Jabari's shoulders shook in amusement. "How did you sleep?" he asked.

"Better than expected. I haven't been camping in years," she replied.

"Nowhere to camp in Manhattan, huh?" he amused.

"The subway," she quipped.

Simone removed her hair tie, and her braids fell around her

face. With both hands, she pulled them back into a ponytail, drawing Jabari's attention to her alluring big brown eyes, cute button nose, and tantalizing full lips.

"You've been busy. How long have you been up?" she asked.

"A couple of hours. I've been enjoying this pleasant morning."

"This is nice," she said.

Jabari took in the surroundings and nodded blissfully. When the fish were ready, he removed them from the fire and placed them on a plastic dish. With a plastic fork, he removed a piece of the meat and fed Simone her first bite. "How does it taste?" he asked.

"Wonderful," she replied.

Jabari was pleased.

As they sat together and enjoyed their morning meal, they also delighted in the idyllic landscape—the dew-covered tree leaves glistening in the morning sun, the sound of the flowing river, and the birds chirping high up in the trees.

"Do you see that cliff over there?" Jabari pointed to a bare piece of rock high up in the hills.

Simone chewed a piece of fish and swallowed before answering, "Yes."

"It's a lookout point. On a clear day, you can see clear across into Tennessee from up there," Jabari said.

"I wish we had time to see it, although I am a little afraid of heights," Simone said.

"I used to be afraid of heights, too," Jabari said.

"You *used* to be?"

"Yes, but I got over it."

"How?" Simone asked.

"When I joined the military, I had to jump out of planes for three years." He removed a fishbone from his mouth and tossed it on the ground.

"Is that all it took?" she asked.

"That's all."

"You think it'd work for me?"

"Worth a try."

"I'll pass. Besides, I'm not afraid of normal heights," she said.

"What are normal heights?"

"You know, anything with a stable platform, but climbing a ladder to clean gutters or rock climbing terrifies me," she said.

"I could help you with the gutters." He flashed his eyebrows. "But no rock climbing for me either."

"There are better ways to die," Simone added.

"Ain't that the truth."

They finished eating and Jabari washed the plates and utensils in the river. He wiped them clean with sanitizer and packed them away. He quickly packed away the rest of his gear and handed Simone his trekking polls. There was a path leading from the river back up to the trail. It wasn't very steep, so they climbed it easily. They traipsed along the narrow path for a while with Simone setting the pace.

"Hi, there," a voice came from nowhere.

They turned and saw four hikers approaching.

"Hi," Jabari said.

A short stout man stepped forward. "I'm Dan, and this pretty lady is Starla." He gestured toward a slim earthy woman with long dirty-blonde hair with pink highlights.

The woman beamed joyfully and held out her hand.

Jabari took her hand in his. "It is nice to meet you."

Another guy, tall and blonde, with his hair pulled into a man bun, extended his hand. "I'm Evan and this is Aleshanee."

A petite young woman with long black hair and a dreamcatcher tattooed on her arm, smiled and waved her hand.

"Nice to meet you, too." Jabari said.

"Likewise."

Simone asked, "Where are you guys from?"

Evan wrapped his arm around Aleshanee's shoulder. "Oklahoma."

"And you?" Jabari asked Dan and Starla.

"Chicago," Dan said.

"No, *he's* from Chicago. I'm from Montreal," Starla interjected.

"We live in Chicago," Dan corrected.

"For now," Starla said.

"I'm from Durham, and as it turns out, so is she. I'm Jabari, by the way."

"I'm Simone."

They all turned and continued hiking.

"Where did you two get on?" Dan asked.

"I got on at Davenport Gap," Jabari answered.

Simone explained, "I got on only a few miles back. My car broke down yesterday afternoon, and Jabari is helping me get to town so I can get it fixed."

"So that was your car back there?" Dan asked.

"Unfortunately, yes."

"We'll get it fixed once we reach Hot Springs," Jabari reassured.

Simone turned to Aleshanee. "How far are you guys going?"

"All the way to Maine."

"Whew. Bless your heart," Simone said.

"We're pretty motivated," Starla assured.

"We don't do anything half-assed," Dan added, drawing a chuckle from Simone.

The trail bent upward for a few hundred yards before leveling off. A six-pointed buck and several does stood grazing atop the hill, feeding on some plants. Evan pulled out his phone and snapped a picture. The buck turned toward the group and sneered as the does and two fawns scurried away. The buck glared at the group before running off.

Evan examined the photo. "Nice," he exclaimed.

The group resumed their trek.

"How did you find yourself stranded way up here?" Aleshanee asked Simone.

"Well, I competed in a mud run with friends over the weekend and decided to spend one extra night and take the scenic route home. I was driving along when my car died," Simone said.

"What's a mud run?" Aleshanee asked.

"Obstacle course racing," Simone replied.

"What sort of obstacles?"

"Climbing ropes, scaling walls, treading through mud pits, crawling under barbed wire, etcetera. It's brutal."

"Sounds like hell," Dan said.

"You have no idea," Jabari interjected.

"And you've done these races before, Jabari?" Aleshanee asked.

"I've done a few."

"Sounds dangerous," Dan said.

"Well, you *do* have to sign a death waiver," Jabari said, and he and Simone laughed and slapped five.

"And you two enjoy this sort of thing?" Starla asked, incredulously.

"I enjoy it better when it's over," Jabari chuckled.

"I've run a few marathons. That's enough for me," Starla said.

"It's a hard no on both," Dan said, smiling.

Starla, his girlfriend, laughed.

"Everything is not for everybody," Jabari said.

"You got that right," Dan concurred.

They soon came to a clearing, and Jabari turned to Simone. "I think we're here." He looked at his map. "The bed-and-breakfast is about a quarter of a mile east." He turned to the group. "If you guys need supplies, there's a grocery store near the bed-and-breakfast."

"We could use a few things," Evan said.

"All right, lead the way," Dan said.

They strolled along the winding road that carried them through the center of Hot Springs. Jabari caught sight of an auto repair shop and pointed it out to Simone. "Maybe they can help us," he said.

"Let's go see," Simone said. The sign above the door read Frazier and Sons.

"It was nice meeting you guys." Simone called out, "Safe travels."

"Good luck with your car," Aleshanee replied.

The group continued into town as Jabari and Simone made their way to the shop and stepped inside. Jabari reached in his bag and handed Simone her keys.

"May I help you?" a young man sitting behind the counter asked. He had blonde hair and hazel eyes.

"Hi, I need a towing service, my car has broken down," Simone said.

"What type of car is it?"

"A blue Honda Accord," Simone said.

"Where's it located?"

"Bluff Mountain Road, right next to the trail crossing. I think my timing belt is broken. Do you think you can fix it?"

"Well, let me get it back to the shop first, and we'll take a look at it," he said. He attached a sheet of paper to a clipboard and handed it to her. "Fill this out please," he asked.

"Sure." She leaned against the counter, her weight settled on one leg, while the other stretched back behind her, heel lifted lightly off the floor.

Jabari stood watching as she filled out the paperwork and handed over her keys.

"What time should I come by?" Simone asked.

"Well, I'll need a few hours to get it back here and see what's wrong with it," he said.

Simone looked at the clock. It was 12:15 P.M. "How does three o'clock sound?"

"That ought to be fine," he said.

"Okay, I'll see you then. Bye-bye."

They stepped outside and strolled along a winding road until they came upon the Oak Tree Inn.

"How charming." Simone admired the idyllic landscaping that appeared to be an accidental force of nature. A giant oak tree stood in the front yard appearing to be at least one hundred years old. Crepe myrtle trees and wildflowers decorated the surrounding hillside.

Simone ran her hand along the large oak tree and looked upon the blooming lavender bushes and lilacs aligning the inn. Two large pillars supported a second-floor balcony, and an old-fashioned swing hung from the porch.

Jabari and Simone entered the building and looked around. The bed-and-breakfast lobby exuded an enchanting Victorian charm, transporting guests to a bygone era of opulence and elegance. Ornate woodwork adorned the walls and plush seating upholstered in rich floral fabrics beckoned them to sit and relax. The focal point of the room was a grand fireplace, adorned with a majestic wooden mantle, showcasing intricate carvings and filigree. The velvety drapes cascading from the ceiling-high windows allowed soft natural light to filter in.

Simone's eyes twinkled as she took in her surroundings.

Jabari leaned over and whispered in her ear, "Wait until you see the gardens."

"Welcome to the Oak Tree Inn," a young woman said from behind the front desk.

She wore a yellow sundress with pink rose petals printed across her abdomen. Her blonde hair hung just below her shoulders.

"Hi, I'm Jabari Miller. I'm sorry, I had a reservation for yesterday, but I didn't make it in time."

"Not a problem. It happens all the time. We have one room left. Would you still like to check in?" she asked.

"Yes, that would be great." Jabari handed her his credit card.

The clerk handed Jabari a pair of keys. "Here you go, Mr. Miller. You're in room two-o-one. I'm Danielle and don't hesitate to call if you need anything. Okay?"

Jabari smiled, "Thank you, Danielle."

"You're welcome, darling."

Simone eyed the small gift shop area and fixed her eyes on a cream-colored Oak Tree Inn t-shirt. "Can I get one of those in a small?" she asked.

"Sure thing," the clerk stepped behind the display of souvenirs and returned with the shirt. "That will be twenty-three, ninety-nine, dear."

"Are there anymore rooms available?" Simone asked.

"I'm afraid not," the clerk answered.

Simone tapped her card on the card reader and slung the shirt over her shoulder. She turned to Jabari, "I hope they can get me back on the road this evening, but I can't be sure."

Jabari nodded. "We'll figure it out." Jabari gestured toward the staircase.

Simone shrugged her shoulders, and they ascended to the second floor.

When he opened the door to the room, he followed Simone inside. He dropped his bag near the wall and looked around the room. The walls were adorned with richly patterned wallpaper featuring intricate floral motifs, perfectly complementing the elegant crown molding and ceiling medallions. A chandelier hung gracefully from the ceiling. The centerpiece of the room was an antique four-poster bed, draped in vintage fabric with lace and tassels cascading down the sides.

Simone sat on the bed and took in her surroundings. Jabari sat in a chair across from her.

Simone rubbed her hands on the bedspread beneath her thighs and said, "This is nice."

"It is," Jabari smiled and nodded.

Simone lay back on the bed and perched her lips. "I'm exhausted."

"Do you want the shower first?"

"You can go first. I just want to lie here for a while," she replied.

"All right. I'll take a shower then."

Simone closed her eyes. "Okay. I'll be here," she murmured.

Jabari pulled himself up from the chair. He pulled his clean clothes and toiletries from his backpack and stepped into the bathroom. As the hot shower massaged his shoulders and warmed his back, Jabari thought about how his trip had unfolded. *I should have been halfway to Walnut Mountain by now. No way I'll make it at this point*, he thought. However, he was feeling good about meeting Simone. She had turned out to be a pleasant surprise.

Jabari stepped out of the shower and dried off. He methodically flossed and brushed his teeth and put on a pair of sweatpants. He looked himself over in the mirror and exited the bathroom. Simone was sleeping on the bed, and he decided not to wake her. He finished dressing and stood at the window, staring out at the horizon and thinking about his upcoming testimony.

Jabari was scheduled to appear in court in a matter of days, set to testify about his role in the shooting of Miles Goodwin, an unarmed teenager. The trial had stretched on for weeks, and Jabari was its central witness. Taking the stand was nothing new for him—he'd done it many times before—but never for something this serious. Protesters had filled the streets of Durham for days on end, and the stress of the case was wearing on his mind. He had planned the weekend trip to get away from it all. He looked over at Simone, who was still sleeping on the bed. He wondered what would've happened had they met under different circumstances. She seemed to like him, and he certainly liked her. His eyes surveyed her face, the shape of her lips and her hourglass physique. *You're not ready for these problems, my dear. Another time perhaps, but not now,* he thought.

Chapter Four

Jabari stood brooding near the window and staring out at the horizon. He crossed the room and powered up his cellular phone, which was charging on the nightstand near the bed. A voicemail message from the district attorney's office awaited him. *"Hi, Officer Miller. This is District Attorney Powell, calling to confirm that you are scheduled in court to testify about the Miles Goodwin case on Thursday. I would like to meet with you and go over a few things first, so please call me at your earliest convenience. Thanks."*

Simone awoke and stirred on the bed. "Is everything all right?"

"All good," Jabari reassured.

Simone sat up and rotated her body until her feet hit the floor. She sat with her toes pointing inward and her hands resting beneath her thighs. "What time is it?" she asked.

"Three o'clock. Are you ready to go?"

"I wanted to take a shower," she said.

"I know, but I thought you needed to rest, so I didn't wake you."

"A girl still needs to wash." She smiled. "I'll pop in the shower and then we can go see about the car. That is if they've towed it in by now."

Jabari stood and crossed the room. He reached into his bag and retrieved her phone.

"Thanks." She reached for the charger and plugged it in.

"There's a new toothbrush in the bathroom," Jabari said.

Simone blew into her hand and sniffed. "Are you trying to tell me something?"

"No, silly," he chuckled.

When Simone stood and crossed the room, Jabari couldn't help but gaze at her alluring figure.

Simone caught his eye in the mirror and Jabari looked away. She entered the bathroom and closed the door.

Jabari heard the shower water running, and he lay back on the bed, crossing his legs while he waited for her to finish.

She eventually stepped out of the bathroom, where Jabari sat waiting. "All ready," she announced.

Jabari sat up and slipped on his shoes.

Simone checked her phone and saw it was only ten percent charged. She pressed her lips and left it charging on the nightstand.

They exited the room, descended the stairs, and stepped out onto the porch.

"Did you say something about a garden?" she asked.

"Yes. It's out back."

"Are you gonna show me?"

"Right this way." He led Simone around the side of the house and into the backyard, stepping into a lush and vibrant oasis, meticulously designed to evoke the charm and grace of the Victorian era. A cobblestone path lined with fragrant roses and butterfly bushes guided them through a green of hidden treasures. The air was filled with the delicate scent of blossoming flowers and the soft rustling of leaves in the breeze.

In the center of the garden stood a fountain adorned with intricate statuary, where water danced gracefully in the sunlight, reflecting the shimmering colors of the surrounding flora. Benches with ornate ironwork invited guests to sit and immerse themselves in the tranquil atmosphere.

Towering old-growth trees provided shade, and their branches created dappled patterns of light and shadow on the ground below, and just beyond the garden, the Spring Creek River glistened in the sunlight. Simone strolled around the garden, sniffing the flowers and beaming with pleasure. She sat on a bench and turned to Jabari. "When were you last here?"

"A few years ago."

She shook her head. "This place isn't at all what I expected."

"What did you expect?"

She shrugged her shoulders. "I don't know. You struck me as a guy who would like something more rustic."

"What gave you that impression?"

She looked him up and down. "Everything."

Jabari sat beside her. "Disappointed?"

"Not at all."

They sat for a while, taking in the surroundings.

"I guess we had better get moving," he said.

Simone looked around the garden. "If we must."

They left the inn and strolled along a winding country road to Frazier and Sons and stepped inside.

"Hi Ms. Morton," the young man sitting behind the counter said.

"Have you picked up my car?"

"Sure did. Just a minute, please." He opened the door to the shop and leaned in. "Papa. Papa, she's here."

A man stepped into the reception area with a full head of gray hair and a graying mustache. "Miss Morton?"

"Yes."

"I'm Russell Frazier. How you do, ma'am?"

"I'm fine. Thank you, Mr. Frazier."

"Call me Russell."

"Russell, is my car ready?"

"No, ma'am, I'm afraid it's going to take a couple of days."

"I don't have a couple of days. I need to get home. Is there any way to fix it sooner?"

"Well, you see, when your timing belt broke, it caused a bit of damage to your engine. I'll have to order some parts, and they won't be in until tomorrow morning."

"Well, how long does it take to replace the timing belt?"

"It's not a matter of time, ma'am, but I have cars in front of yours, you see."

"Listen Russell, I don't mean to be pushy, but my car broke down yesterday afternoon. No one would stop and help me, and I sat out in the sun for hours before this gentleman here came along. He's a hiker on the trail and agreed to accompany me to town and help me get my car fixed," her voice cracked, and she let out a long breath. "Well, on the way, the bridge was closed, and we had to sleep outside in a tent. We didn't make it to town until this morning when I came by. Please understand, Russell, I am tired, and I need to get home."

"Where're you from?"

"Durham," Simone answered.

Russell stroked his chin. "I'll try to have you on the road by tomorrow evening, but I can't make any promises, you see."

"That would be great," Simone said, and dabbed at the corners of her eyes.

"Have you found anywhere to stay?"

"We're at the Oak Tree Inn," Jabari said.

"That's a good place. I'll call you when it's ready, Ms. Morton."

"Thank you, Russell. Call me Simone."

Jabari shook Russell's hand and said, "I'm Jabari."

"It's a pleasure," Russell said.

"Can we get her bags from the car?"

"Oh yes, right this way." Russell led them into the work area.

Simone opened the car door and pulled her bag from the back seat. She sat it on its wheels and extended the handle.

"I'll take that," Jabari said.

They turned toward the door and exited the shop.

They strolled along the road until they came upon Andrews Street, where there were several shops and eateries and a steady flow of patrons looking for supplies and good food.

"Did we miss something?" Jabari pointed to several parade floats which were left on the side of the road. And multiple vendors stood under canopies selling various trinkets and souvenirs.

"I hope not."

Strolling past Big Pillow Brewing, Jabari peered into the outdoor seating area, where dozens of customers sat at wooden picnic tables, shaded by green umbrellas and string lights flowing overhead. He noticed a man with a familiar blonde man bun sitting next to a petite young woman with long jet-black hair and olive skin. He recognized the couple as Evan and Aleshanee. The pudgy man sitting across from them locked eyes with Jabari and waved him inside. Jabari turned to Simone. "Are you up for a drink?"

"Sure."

Jabari and Simone stepped into the outdoor seating area. "Hey, guys. I was hoping we'd find you," Aleshanee said, through grinning teeth.

Starla scooted over and they sat down at the table.

Dan slid a basket of tortilla chips toward them and waved over the waiter.

Jabari popped a chip in his mouth and turned to Simone. "What would you like?"

She looked over the menu. "The Appalachian Fog Hazy matches the mood I'm in, so I'll have that."

Jabari let out a chuckle.

A bearded man with sleeve tattoos stepped over and asked Jabari, "What are you drinking?"

"The Appalachian Fog Hazy for the lady, and I'll have the Blue Mountain Porter," Jabari ordered.

The waiter nodded and stepped over to the open bar.

Simone turned to Starla. "What's going on out here?"

Starla held up her beer in a salutary fashion. "It's Trail Fest," she declared.

Dan, Evan, and Aleshanee followed suit and repeated, "Trail Fest."

The two couples all took large gulps of beer and slammed down their mugs.

"It's on you," Dan said to Evan. "Out of the trails you've completed, which trail was your favorite? And what trail is highest on your to-do list?"

"Okay." Evan rubbed his chin thoughtfully. "The trail I'd like to do most of all is Kungsleden in Sweden. But my favorite trail I've hiked thus far was the Curry Ridge Trail in Denali State Park, Alaska. It's only a six-and-a-half-mile hike, but the views are fucking amazing."

"You mean the trail where we almost died?" Aleshanee asked.

"Well, besides that, yes," Evan answered.

Laughter spread around the table.

"Babe, show them some of your pictures from Curry Ridge," Evan said.

Aleshanee pulled out her phone and showed them several photos of the trail.

"How did you almost die?" Starla asked.

Evan took a sip of his beer. "We camped a few days at the K'esugi Ken Campground and fished on the lake, and Aleshanee did her photography thing. So, we're down by the lake fishing and this fucking grizzly comes out and just sat staring at us."

Aleshanee swiped through a few more photos that showed the grizzly bear that looked to be at least four hundred pounds.

Simone covered her mouth. "Holy shit," she exclaimed.

The waiter returned and placed their beers in front of them. "Anything to eat?" he asked.

"Tequila shrimp tacos," Simone ordered.

"And you, sir?"

Jabari turned to Aleshanee. "What's that you're eating?"

"Carnitas," she answered.

Jabari turned back to the waiter. "What kind of meat is in the Carnitas?"

"It's pork shoulder."

Jabari pressed his lips. "Well, in that case, I'll have the apple chian chicken tacos and nachos for the table" he said.

"Not a fan of pork?" Simone asked, with a raised eyebrow.

"Not since the Army. No red meat either."

"Is it a religious thing?" she asked.

"No. I just needed to get in shape and make it through boot camp, and I never went back to it."

Evan continued his story, "Finally, after what seemed like an eternity, the bear stood and moved toward us." Evan took another drink of beer and raised his arms over his head. "So, Aleshanee played dead, and the other guys and I raised our hands in the air and stared it down, and finally the bear charged at us. So, one of the guys we were with started screaming and charged the bear. I didn't know what to do, so I charged behind him until the bear turned and trotted off toward the lake."

"Why didn't you run?" Simone asked.

Jabari turned to Simone. "Never run from a bear."

"Why not?"

"Because if you do, the bear's instinct is to chase you down, and you can't outrun a bear," Jabari said.

"Dude, if I hadn't just taken a dump an hour ago, I would've shit my pants," Evan said, leading to another outbreak of laughter.

"There's more to the story," Aleshanee announced.

"At that point, I felt we were the baddest dudes in Alaska," Evan said.

"Until later on that night," Aleshanee interjected with a pointed finger.

"Right. So, sometime in the wee hours of the morning, Aleshanee wakes me up, her eyes big as saucers. She leans over and whispers, there's something outside."

"Oh, Lord." Simone leaned forward, listening intently.

The waiter returned to the table and placed the tacos and nachos on the table. "Another drink?" the waiter asked.

Jabari pointed down at the table and whipped his finger in a circular motion. "Another round for the table."

Dan held up his glass toward Jabari. "Thanks, buddy."

Jabari gave him a thumbs up and refocused his attention on Evan's story.

"We hear this deep snorting and grunting sound outside of our tent."

"Oh, fuck, it was terrible." Aleshanee shook her head and dropped her face into her palms.

"And then it came closer, and we could see the bear's shadow outside the tent. I swear, he knew it was us."

"Oh, God." Starla placed her hand over her heart.

"Finally, it meandered over to the trash and rummaged through it."

"Thank God for whatever idiot had left the trash bin open," Aleshanee said.

"Better the trash than us," Evan said.

"What did you do?" Starla asked.

"Nothing. We stayed silent and prayed it didn't notice us," Aleshanee said.

"Well, did it?" Simone asked, before biting into a taco.

"Thank God it didn't. It eventually wandered off," Evan answered.

"And when the sun rose, we got the hell out of there," Aleshanee said.

More laughter erupted around the table.

"It's still my favorite trail," Evan said.

"My favorite was the Inca Trail to Machu Picchu," Starla said. She pulled up some pictures on her phone and passed it around the table. Starla appeared in several photos smiling on a hill above the Inca ruins.

"Nice!" Evan exclaimed.

Jabari reached for the phone so he and Simone could flip through the photos before passing the phone back to Starla.

"And at the top of my bucket list." Starla gazed across the courtyard, thoughtfully. "I would have to say the Kalalau Trail in Hawaii."

"And you, Jabari," Aleshanee asked.

Jabari chewed his apple chian chicken tacos and washed it down with beer. "I've only done trails within North Carolina, and the Appalachian Trail will always be my favorite for sentimental reasons, and at the of top my bucket list would be the Whale Trail in South Africa."

"Oh yes, I would love to see that," Aleshanee said.

"What is there to see, exactly?" Simone asked.

Jabari turned to Simone. "Every year, between June and November, hundreds of Southern Right Whales breed off the coast of South Africa. The Whale Trail is a six-day hike along the coast where you could watch the whales breeding and giving birth near the shore."

"That does sound exciting," Simone smiled.

Outside the brewery, festivalgoers filled the streets. "Who's ready to see what this festival is all about?" Jabari asked.

Dan downed the rest of his beer. "Let's do it."

Jabari signaled the waiter for the checks. He opened his wallet and pulled out enough cash to cover the tab for himself and Simone. His Durham PD badge sparkled in the sunlight.

"Are you a cop?" Dan asked.

"I am." Jabari nodded and put away his wallet. He settled the bill and joined the group as they made their way from the outdoor dining area toward the street.

"Wait a minute. Over here." Dan led the group over to the side bar and slammed down his credit card. "Six shots of tequila," he called to the bartender.

Simone let out a deep breath. "Oh, Lord. He's trying to get us shitfaced," she whispered to Jabari.

The group stood around the bar and waited on the bartender to pour the drinks.

Two flat-screen televisions hung on the wall behind the bar. One television was tuned to the Appalachian State Mountaineers softball team playing against the Virginia Tech Hokies. Simone took a seat and focused on the game while Jabari chatted with the group.

Jabari felt Simone tapping him on the shoulder.

"Look." She pointed to the television where the local news station had cut into the game. Bold red letters flashed across the screen. *BREAKING NEWS.*

Simone called to the bartender. "Hey. Will you turn that up please?"

"Breaking News from Durham. We are live on the scene in Chavis Park, where protesters of the Miles Goodwin shooting have taken down Old Gray Glory," the newswoman said.

Jabari's stomach tightened, as the group turned their attention to the news announcement.

Chapter Five

After the breaking-news announcement, the camera cut away from the newswoman to a sizable group of protesters marching along East Main Street as they chanted, *"No racist cops, no KKK, no fascist U-S-A. No racist cops, no KKK, no fascist U-S-A."* Passing Old Gray Glory, a confederate soldier's monument, a protester hurled a bottle into the face of the nameless soldier. The bottle exploded and purple liquid covered the monument. The protesters turned their attention toward the statue.

"Take it down. Take it down," they chanted.

A protester climbed on top of the obelisk and tied a rope around the statue. He tossed the other end down and a group of protesters pulled at it.

The crowd continued chanting, *"Take it down. Take it down."*

A group of protesters pulled until the statue tilted forward and fell to the ground, just before the crowd erupted in cheers, then kicking and spitting upon the statue. They poured liquids on it and beat it with sticks, seeming to take out all their frustrations against the history of racism and segregation, and against every microaggression they had ever experienced. The protesters triumphantly dragged the statue through the street and left it at the door of the Durham County Court House.

"Holy shit, is that where you live?" Dan asked Jabari.

"Yes, that's happening in Durham," Jabari said.

"What are they so mad about?" Dan asked.

"A police shooting," Jabari answered.

Dan shook his head and clinched his fists. "I want you to know, Jabari, that I completely back the Blue." Dan announced, "Those protesters can go to hell."

"It's not always that simple, Dan," Simone said.

"Sure, it is," Dan countered, his face turning red.

Simone pressed her lips and let out a deep breath. "Every case is unique, needing to be evaluated on its own merits. Far too often, people choose sides before knowing any of the facts, but we should never jump to conclusions about guilt or innocence without first weighing all the facts objectively."

Jabari watched Starla, standing shoulder to shoulder with Simone, cross her arms and glare at Dan, but Dan didn't seem to notice. Dan opened his mouth to respond to Simone, but Jabari interjected before he could speak, "You're absolutely right, Simone, and Dan, I appreciate your support, but can we please change the subject?"

"Yes, of course." Dan turned away.

Jabari watched as Starla pulled Dan to the side and fussed at him in hushed tones before he folded his arms and lowered his head.

Flashbacks from the night of the shooting filled Jabari's mind. He saw himself standing over Miles Goodwin's lifeless body, staring down at him. Jabari felt Simone place her hand on his arm. She rubbed and squeezed it briefly, before letting go. Her touch pulled his mind back from the dreadful night. He turned to Simone. "I've always hated that fucking statue. I've never stepped foot in that park because of it, but that wasn't the right way to get rid of it."

"They've been trying to do it the right way for years, but they've been denied," Simone said.

Jabari didn't respond.

The bartender brought over the shot glasses and filled them with tequila. The sight of the clear liquor seemed to raise Dan's spirits.

The group held up their glasses as Dan shouted, "To Trail Fest."

The group followed suit and shouted together, "Trail Fest."

They downed their shots and strolled out onto Andrews Street where a crowd of festivalgoers filled the street. They weaved in and out of boutiques, souvenir stores, and antique shops aligning Andrews Street and Bridge Street.

"This looks interesting," Starla said, leading the group into the Iron Horse Station Artison Gallery, a gift shop offering handcrafted souvenirs and keepsakes.

"Welcome," a young lady said, as they entered the building.

"Thank you," Starla said, as she wandered around the store examining the eccentric collection of trinkets, souvenirs, pictures, books, and jewelry.

"I wouldn't know what to do with this stuff," Dan said.

"It's charming, don't you think?" Starla said.

"Yes, it is," Simone agreed, as she sniffed scented candles.

"Too bad I can't carry any of this in my backpack," Starla said.

"I'm not sure I would want to," Dan said.

Simone and Jabari proceeded to the back row and looked over the pottery and glazed stones.

Jabari asked her, "See anything you like?"

"I see plenty, but I don't want to carry any of it back to the inn," Simone said.

They looked around some more before heading back toward the door.

Simone faced Jabari. "May I ask you a personal question?" she said, looking up at him.

"Sure."

"You mentioned you're on administrative leave," Simone began, cautiously. "I hope you don't mind me asking... but were you involved in the Miles Goodwin shooting?"

Jabari dropped his gaze, his shoulders tense. After a moment, he looked up and met her eyes. "Yes, I was."

"Are you the one who shot him?"

He shook his head. "No. I didn't pull the trigger, but I was on the scene when it happened."

Simone hesitated, then asked quietly, "Is that why you're here? Trying to get away from the protests since the bodycam footage came out?"

"Not entirely," he replied. "I was already planning this trip before it was released. But... yeah, putting some space between me and all that noise back home hasn't been the worst thing."

Simone's eyes welled with emotion. "I'm sorry," she murmured. "I shouldn't have brought it up." She turned away quickly and stepped outside. Finding a nearby bench, she took a seat, wringing her hands.

Jabari followed her outside, wanting to explain what happened. He sat next to her, searching for the words to explain, but before he could, Aleshanee and Evan came over and sat with them.

"Is everything okay?" Aleshanee asked.

Simone wiped her eyes and smiled, "Oh yes, I'm fine."

Starla and Dan came shortly after, and the group meandered around the town some more.

Dan raised his head and sniffed the air. "Do y'all smell that?"

"What?" Simone asked.

"Oh, my God, they have a Kilwins," Dan said.

"The ice cream shop?" Simone asked.

Dan surveyed the group. "Have you guys never had Kilwins?"

Simone shook her head no.

"You are about to think you died and gone to heaven. Come on," he said, hurrying toward the shop. He pulled open the door and the smell of fresh waffle cones and chocolate filled the air.

Simone's face lit up with a look of pure pleasure.

Dan smiled at her kid-like. "What did I tell you?" He proceeded to the counter. "Six waffle cones please. One with chocolate chip cookie dough, one with chocolate, and what do you want, dear?" Dan asked Simone.

"Butter pecan, please," she answered.

Jabari, Evan, and Aleshanee needed time to decide. While they hovered over the flavor board, Dan stepped up, handed over his credit card, and waited.

Once their waffle cones were ready, they all crossed the street together and found a bench in the park.

"This is where all my allowance went when I was a kid— my waistline too," Dan said with a grin.

Simone laughed, and Jabari couldn't help but smile.

Dan turned to Starla, "No Kilwins in Canada," he teased.

"Ha, ha," Starla replied.

"Are you really moving back to Canada?" Simone asked Starla.

"The first chance I get."

"What's stopping you?" Simone asked.

"My career and Dan," Starla said.

"Life has a way of deciding for you if you let it," Simone said.

"So true." Starla took a long lick of her chocolate ice cream.

"It's nice up there. I understand why you miss it." Simone caught the butter pecan oozing down the side of her cone with her tongue.

"You've been?" Starla asked.

"A few times."

"Where?"

"Toronto and Niagara-on-the-lake, which was so amazing," Simone answered.

"Niagara-on-the-lake is my happy place." Starla smiled.

"I didn't want to leave, but I'm a southern girl, and I'm not sure I could handle those winters," Simone said.

"Oh, you get used to it."

"Some places are better to visit," Simone said, laughing.

Starla laughed.

"What's going on over there?" Evan pointed toward the bridge where dozens of festivalgoers gathered and peered down at the water.

"Let's go see," Dan said.

They stood and made their way over to the bridge. "Ahh, a duck race," Jabari said, and pointed to a banner which read, "18th Annual Rubber Duck Race."

Peering over the bridge, the group saw other festivalgoers standing by the riverbank, rubber ducks in hand.

"Get your ducks here," a young man yelled from a table.

"Oh, I'm game," Simone announced, and trotted toward the table of rubber ducks. Evan and Aleshanee joined her by the table just as Simone called to Jabari, "You coming?"

Jabari, Dan, and Starla stepped over.

"There's no way your rubber duckie can beat mine," Jabari said.

"Are you kidding me? I'm well experienced at this," Simone countered.

"Really? You have experience racing rubber ducks?" he said, amused.

"Haven't you ever raced a paper boat down the street after a storm?" Simone asked.

"No."

"That's why you're gonna lose." Simone turned toward the table. She pulled ten dollars from her bag and bought rubber ducks for her and Jabari. She picked up a marker and wrote her name on the side.

"First place wins seven hundred and fifty chamber dollars, which can be used anywhere in town," the young man at the table said. The rest of the group bought their rubber ducks and rushed over to the riverbank, where two men stood in the river, holding back hundreds of rubber duckies with a large net.

"Whoever comes in last place, buys a round of drinks for everyone," Dan announced.

"What does the winner get?" Simone asked.

"Free drinks all night," Dan said.

Soon the festivalgoers counted down. "Five, four, three, two, one." The two men in the river lifted the net out of the water and the rubber duckies began racing downstream. Dozens of kids jumped in the river and chased the ducks toward the finish line. Aleshanee's duck took the early lead amongst their group. Simone's duck traveled closely behind. They shuffled along the riverbank cheering on the rubber ducks.

When Jabari's duck stalled near a branch, he yelled out, "Seriously." He saw Simone and Aleshanee gaining distance. He placed Simone's bag on the ground and reached for the branch and pulled it out of the water, freeing his duck to move downstream, but not before Dan and Starla's ducks moved ahead of his. His duck was now running neck and neck with Evan's. He picked up Simone's bag and continued alongside of it. His duck moved into a swift current and picked up speed. His duck soon moved past Dan and Starla's, and was running in third place, when he looked ahead and saw Simone and Aleshanee's ducks moving past the finish line and Simone pumping her fist.

"Yes. I told you!" She beamed.

Jabari's duck crossed the finish line and he turned to see Dan's and Starla's right behind his. He saw Evan far behind peering into the water. Evan slapped his hands together and shook his head, before moping over to join the group.

"Where's your duck?" Jabari asked Evan.

"I don't know. I lost sight of it halfway into the race."

"Sucks to be you," Simone held up her rubber duck triumphantly.

"Drinks on Evan," Dan announced.

Across the field a band stood on a small stage playing bluegrass music. Dozens of festivalgoers sat listening. The three couples strolled over to the band and found seats.

As Evan sat, Dan turned to him and raised his hands. "What are you doing? You need to go and get us a case of beer."

"Get moving," Aleshanee pointed.

"Evan shook his head and moped up the hill toward the street.

The sun was dipping behind the mountain range in the distance while they sat chatting and listening to the band singing over an assortment of banjos, accordions, drums and tambourines. Evan returned with a case of Samuel Adams and passed them around.

"I found your profile," Starla said to Simone.

"I hope you sent a friend request."

"I did, but you didn't tell us you're an author."

"I am." Simone smiled.

"She didn't tell me either," Jabari interjected.

"Two books, is it?" Starla asked.

"That's right."

"What are they about?" Aleshanee asked.

"Personal finance," Simone said.

"Let's see," Starla said, pulling out her phone, "*Financial Planning for Your Future Family and Debt Is the Root of All Evil*," Starla read, and then added, "Good reviews."

"Good reviews, but not enough sales," Simone said.

"People don't like being told how to spend their money," Dan said.

"It was written for a niche market," Simone winked.

"Is debt really the root of all evil?" Dan challenged.

"In most cases, yes."

"Debt can be useful if it is properly managed," Dan said.

"And that's just it, Dan, most people are terrible at managing it. I concede that debt is useful when buying a home or starting a business, but I see no other use for it," Simone said.

"But don't you think," Dan began, before Starla cut him off.

"Dan, enough already," she said, rolling her eyes.

Jabari placed his hand on Dan's shoulder. "Perhaps you should read the book, before you criticize it, buddy."

Dan whipped out his phone. "I'm buying a copy right now," he said.

"Appreciate it." Simone grinned halfheartedly.

"I'll write a proper review," Dan assured.

"I'm sure you will." Simone let out a deep breath.

"Where are you guys staying?" Jabari asked, changing the subject.

Evan pointed across the field, where two dozen tents surrounded a campfire.

"Cool."

Dan stretched his legs and crossed his feet. "We'll hit the trail again first thing in the morning."

Jabari took a swig of beer. "What's your timeline for reaching Maine?"

"Early October, I hope. Any later, it will be too cold to enjoy," Starla said.

"I wish I could go with you guys, but I have to get back home," Jabari said, wearily.

Starla, with blonde hair cascading down her back, gently brushed it away and massaged her neck. "I would love to take a dip in the healing hot springs before we leave. Do you happen to know how we can access it?"

Jabari turned to Starla. "You can't really. Not unless you stay at the Hot Springs Resort and Spa."

"That's unfortunate," Simone said.

"Legend has it, there is another source to the hot springs beneath Paint Rock, but I don't know anyone who's ever found it," Jabari said.

Aleshanee perked up and gazed at Jabari. "Did you say Paint Rock? Are we near it?"

"Yeah. It's only a six-mile hike from here."

"How did I not know that?" Aleshanee said.

"What's Paint Rock?" Simone asked.

"A Native American heritage site. My dad took me there when I was a kid," Jabari explained.

Aleshanee nodded. "Yes. The Cherokee Nation painted pictographs on the side of the mountain over five thousand years ago. The remnants of the murals are still visible today," Aleshanee explained.

"What Nation are you?" Simone asked.

"My people are Cheyenne."

"Babe. We gotta go. Right?" Evan said.

"Yes," Aleshanee agreed.

"Yeah. Let's do it," Dan said.

"Okay. We can go in the morning," Jabari suggested.

"Do you know the way?" Aleshanee asked.

Jabari nodded. "I believe the trail starts on the other side of the river. It's about a three-hour hike."

"Should we meet you guys back here around nine A.M.?" Simone suggested.

"Nine A.M.," Evan confirmed.

Jabari stood. "Okay then. We'll see you back here in the morning. He grabbed Simone's bag, and they climbed the hill back up to the road. "Are you up for it?" Jabari asked her.

"Yeah. It sounds interesting."

"I just thought maybe you'd had enough of Dan," Jabari smiled.

Simone chuckled. "I like all of them, but I can only handle Dan in small increments."

"Exactly." Strolling along Andrews Street, Jabari noticed a general store. "I should run in there and grab a few things."

"Okay."

They stepped inside and Jabari restocked on batteries, power bars, and trail mix.

"What sort of wine do you like, Jabari?"

"I like reds."

"Good answer," she said, before picking up a bottle of Pinot Noir. They stepped into the night and headed back to the inn. They strolled along the dark curvy road, listening to the sounds of the country after dark, an orchestra of crickets, bullfrogs and cicadas.

Jabari gazed up at the night sky. "I wish we could see the stars like this back home."

"Oh, yeah. Do you know what I wish I could see?"

"What?"

"Northern Lights. One day, I'm going to Iceland to see it." Simone stared at the starlit sky with Jabari.

"That sounds nice," Jabari said.

They made it back to the Oak Tree Inn and climbed onto the porch. Jabari pushed open the door and they stepped inside.

Passing the receptionist, Jabari asked, "Do you have a roll-away bed available?"

"No, I'm sorry," the receptionist answered.

"It's cool—just make sure you stay on your side of the bed," Simone said, over her shoulder.

"Scout's honor," Jabari said.

The two ascended the stairs and entered the room. They sat and chatted for a while before Simone pulled clean shorts and a t-shirt from her bag and went for the shower.

"Back in a few," she said.

Jabari leaned back on the headboard of the bed and nodded.

Chapter Six

Jabari uncorked the wine with his Swiss Army knife and filled two glasses. He sat on the bed, waiting for Simone to finish her shower. He sipped his wine and wondered about Simone. He liked her in every way a man could like a woman, but he knew his involvement in the shooting worried her. He sat thinking of how he could explain it all.

Simone exited the bathroom wearing a pair of nylon shorts and a t-shirt. Her braided hair hung over her shoulders. She moved across the room and sat across from him near the window.

"Feel better?" he asked her.

"Definitely," she said, reaching for her glass.

"Good."

"These couple of days have been nice. I've enjoyed myself, despite being stranded."

"So have I."

"It was nice to get away and decompress, even if I didn't plan it that way." She sighed. "And I'm sorry if I ruined the weekend you had planned."

"You haven't ruined anything. I'm sorry about your car, but I'm glad I met you."

"I'm glad I met you, too." Simone peered out of the window. "I need to get away more often."

"When was your last vacation?"

"It's been way too long," she said.

"I used to give vacation time back every year, but not anymore. Life's too short."

"Amen to that," she responded.

They sat silently for a while, both enjoying the mountain air blowing into the room through the open window. The moon was full, hanging low over the mountainous landscape. The window framed the moon over one of Simone's shoulders, illuminating her face.

"I'm sorry to bring this up again, but I feel like I need to know what happened. Will you tell me about it—the shooting?"

Jabari took a long sip from his glass, sighed, and nodded. "It was a normal evening. I was riding along South Roxboro Street when I received a call from dispatch, alerting me to a stabbing on Corcoran Street, near the statue of Major the Bull. All I knew was that the suspect was last seen heading toward the Carolina Theater. According to dispatch, he was wearing blue jeans and a white, bloodstained shirt, and he was still holding the knife used in the attack.

"I sped through downtown, toward the Carolina Theater and slowed down, looking for the suspect. I heard screaming, and that's when I saw Miles Goodwin trotting across the campus of the Carolina Theater. I approached and watched him turn and head toward the Durham Arts Counsel. I pulled alongside him and got out of my car, ordering him to drop the knife he was carrying. He continued, and I trotted alongside him, pointing my firearm. I again ordered him to drop it. He stopped and turned to face me, looking wild-eyed. I saw his swollen face and bloody nose, and it appeared that the blood on his white shirt was his own."

Jabari took in a long deep breath before continuing, "He held out the knife and backed up toward the parking deck of the Durham Chamber of Commerce. At that point, I knew he was just a scared kid who had gotten into some sort of trouble. I holstered my firearm and pulled out my taser, holding it down by my side. I asked him to look at me. I met his eyes, and told him it was okay, but I needed him to drop the knife. He lowered the knife to his side but held on to it. I asked him again to let it go. He stood frozen for a moment. I pleaded with him to let it go. I watched him loosen his grip on the knife, and as it fell to the ground, Officer Smith arrived.

"He hopped out of his squad car and approached him from Miles' side. Miles spun around to face him, and Smith fired multiple shots into his chest. I watched the bullets striking him, and I screamed at Smith to stop. I ran toward Miles and knelt beside him. I looked into his eyes and saw a scared boy struggling to breathe. I called for an ambulance and tore open his shirt and started chest compressions, but by the time emergency services arrived and took over, it was too late. Miles Goodwin was already dead."

Simone sat listening, her eyes wide and piercing.

"Have you seen the video?" Jabari asked her.

"No, I haven't. I don't think I want to."

"You should probably see it for yourself." Jabari reached for his phone, which was charging on the nightstand. He found the recording from his bodycam recorder and handed it to her.

Simone watched it happen just as Jabari had described. She slammed the phone down and lowered her head.

"Are you okay?" he asked.

"I told you I didn't want to see it," she said, with her voice cracking.

Jabari sighed and refilled their glasses.

"What happens now?" she asked, just above a whisper.

"The trial should be wrapping up soon, and I'm scheduled to testify against Smith next week."

"Will you?"

"I don't really have a choice."

"What will you say?"

"My truth."

"What's your truth?"

"I can only describe it exactly as it happened from my own perspective—I can't speak to what Officer Smith perceived."

"The video is clear, Jabari. Miles Goodwin was complying when Smith executed that boy. Anyone can see that."

"Smith claims he didn't know Goodwin had dropped the knife, and when Goodwin turned toward him, he thought his life was in danger, so he fired."

"Do you believe that?" Simone pressed, "If that was the case, why didn't you shoot him?"

"I didn't see a need to use force. I thought I could get him to comply. But again, that was my perception. Smith perceived it otherwise, and it's the officer's perception that dictates any use of force."

Simone took a gulp of wine and slammed down her glass. "That is bullshit, Jabari. Because it's the officer's perception that keeps getting us killed."

"I get that, but in this case, the video speaks for itself. I'll testify to what I experienced and how I perceived it. That is all."

"Do you think it was justified?"

"That's up to interpretation. In my view, the shooting wasn't necessary, but justification is left to the interpretation of police policy and training. In the end, it will be left to the jury to decide."

"Do we know why he had the knife?"

"Surveillance videos show him walking along West Parish Street when a group of teenagers attacked him near the statue of Major the Bull. As they beat him, he pulled out a pocketknife and stabbed one of them in the leg before running off," Jabari said.

"Sounds like self-defense."

"It was, but we didn't know that at the time. All we knew was that he had stabbed someone and was running through the streets, still holding a knife. We didn't know his intentions."

Simone sat with crossed arms and glassy eyes.

They sat for a while, finishing the bottle of wine.

"Are you up for seeing Paint Rock tomorrow?" she asked.

"Sure, what else do we have to do?"

Simone set her empty glass on the table. "You don't necessarily have to stay here. You could get on with your hike."

"I'll make sure your car is taken care of before I go," he said.

Simone nodded. "I'd better get some sleep, I suppose."

"Go ahead, I'm gonna sit up for a while."

"Okay, good night then," she said.

As she passed by, Jabari reached for her hand and gazed into her teary eyes. He reached up and wiped a tear from her face. He felt her hands caressing his cheeks. He wrapped his arms around her and pulled her in close. Their lips met during a delicate, affectionate embrace. He pulled her in closer, tasting her tongue and sucking her lips. They climbed into bed and made love.

Later, they lay next to each other in the moonlit room.

Simone turned to Jabari, resting her chin on his chest. "I'm sorry if I pressed you too much earlier. I know it must be difficult for you."

He wrapped his arm around her and squeezed her gently. "It's difficult, especially with all the protests going on. But I welcome the public scrutiny. I believe change is needed, and like-minded officers must stay on to see it through."

"How many officers do you consider like-minded?"

"Many of us believe in police reform. Much more than many may believe. We've had some tough conversations about the use of deadly force, but core beliefs are hard to change."

"Have the so-called like-minded officers tried to educate them on the matter?"

"All the time, but it's not a conversation they're comfortable having, and it is tough, because these are people who would literally die for me—without hesitation they would, but sometimes they say things that make my blood boil."

"I'm sure they'd die for you, as long as you are on their team, but as soon as you step off the reservation, you're on your own," Simone suggested. She rolled onto her back and folded her arms.

"I know that since I don't meet their stereotypical impressions of Black men as a whole, it is easier for many of them to think of me as the exception, rather than to reevaluate their biased beliefs."

"I face the same thing in academia. I feel like I'm everyone's token Black friend," Simone said.

"I know exactly what you mean." He rolled onto his side and faced her. "Now may I ask *you* a personal question?"

"What would you like to know?" she asked in reply.

"You mentioned being homesick in New York, and that being the reason for coming back home, but I can't help but feel there might've been more to it. You seemed to be doing well there with a great job and good opportunities. So, who or what compelled you to leave?"

She paused briefly before answering, "I was actually engaged to be married, but things didn't work out."

"What led to the relationship not working out?"

"A combination of factors," Simone explained. "He loved me, but I didn't feel like he was *in love* with me. There's a difference, you know. I think he only proposed to me due to pressure from his parents. If it weren't for that pressure, I'm not entirely sure he would have proposed at all.

"Tyler and I crossed paths during my first semester in graduate school at Columbia, while I was playing in an intramural soccer league on campus."

Jabari was curious. "Did you play soccer in high school?"

"Yes, and undergrad at Spelman, but this league was coed, and student organized. Anyway, it was obvious he was mustering up the courage to talk to me, so I made it easy for him. As he guarded me on the field, I looked into his eyes and gave him a smile. I casually mentioned recognizing him from my economics class.

"We met the very next day and had a long conversation before heading to class together. In the middle of the lecture, he leaned over and asked me out for a drink, and that's when our dating began. We were practically inseparable from that point on. His parents were both professors at Columbia, and they were our kind of people, if you know what I mean," she said with air quotes.

"The bourgeois type?"

"Exactly." She chuckled. "They were a wonderful family. We really clicked, and his mother became like my unofficial mentor. She introduced me to her colleagues, and I even shared my articles with them.

"After grad school, I landed a teaching job at Westbury University. Meanwhile, Tyler had a tough time finding work and settled for a position at a community college. It wasn't his ideal job, but it was a start, and we were both content doing what we loved. Since Tyler taught evening classes, I dedicated my evenings to working on my first book. When it was finally published, it received a warm reception from its intended audience. I started getting invitations to speak at events and local news outlets to discuss the book. Not long after, Columbia University offered me a position, and it felt like everything was falling into place just as I had envisioned. I hoped Tyler would share in my joy, but instead, he seemed more envious than happy for me. I knew he wasn't satisfied with his teaching job, but I believed he had ample time to progress, but sometimes I felt like he was in competition with me or something," she furrowed her brow.

"His parents took us out to celebrate my new position at Columbia, which I knew they had advocated for me behind the scenes, but they denied having anything to do with it. That's when they first started talking about having grandkids. His mother asked when he was going to marry me—his father asked him what the hell he was waiting on.

"I lit up at the thought of getting married, but Tyler only shrugged his shoulders and drank more wine. That's when I first knew something was terribly wrong in our relationship. His drinking had increased—he worked late a lot and was going out with his colleagues for drinks after work. I didn't mind it much, because it gave me time to work on my second book, which took me about a year to complete. The second book was well received, too—even made it on *Good Morning America*. The funny thing is, I'm not sure if Tyler ever read either one. He was still working late and going out for drinks with colleagues when I was looking for him to become more settled."

Jabari lay beside her listening intently.

"Anyhow, not too long after that, my worst fears became a reality, and I discovered he was involved with someone," Simone shared.

"Who was it?" Jabari inquired.

"A woman from the community college where he taught."

"A student?" Jabari questioned.

"No, a staff member in the admissions office, I think."

"How did you find out?"

Simone shook her head. "That's a story for another time."

Jabari nodded. "Fair enough."

"I stayed the next three nights with my girl, Stacey. Tyler had left numerous messages on my cell and on Stacey's voice-mail. He cried and pleaded for me to return, but I ignored his pleas. A few days later, while Tyler was at work, I went to the apartment with a moving company and removed all my belongings. I settled into an apartment in Harlem. I continued working the way I always had, but I just wanted to get the hell out of there.

"Before that happened, everything in my life seemed perfect. Everything was going just as I had imagined it would. It was my first adult relationship, and I never considered he would do me like that. Looking back on it, I understand we were too young to be so seriously involved, but my parents were young when they married, and so were my grandparents. It seemed natural to me."

"Was it difficult to work around his parents after that?"

"Well, they were in different departments, so I didn't see them much. It seemed like they were avoiding me after that. And I knew they would side with their son, anyway. They were that kind of family, careful to manage a scandal. When the job at NCCU became available, I jumped at the opportunity and came home."

Jabari turned on his side and faced her. "Do you still feel leaving him was the right decision?"

Her response was firm, "No relationship should be that difficult, and I was not about to put up with that shit. And, as for coming home, I'm confident I made the right decision."

"I'm sorry that happened to you, but I'm glad you came

back home. Otherwise, I wouldn't have met you." Jabari ran his thumb over her lips and his eyes surveyed the shape of her body underneath the white bedsheets. He took in the shape of her breasts, which sat up like two snow-capped peaks. With a gentle gesture, he peeled back the sheets and ran his hands over her caramel skin, admiring every part of her toned physique, and a sensation surged through him, arousing his desires. Drawing her close, he pressed his lips against hers, feeling her body relax in his embrace. The world seemed to fade away as they melted into each other's embrace, two souls finding solace in each other's presence.

Simone rolled on top of him. Her braids falling around his face as she gazed at him with her big brown eyes. She brought her lips down to his and her tongue swirled inside his mouth as she slowly took him in.

Chapter Seven

Jabari and Simone awoke the next morning with their arms wrapped around each other, their legs intertwined, and her head nestled in his chest. They no longer wanted to see Paint Rock. They wanted to stay in bed—to be alone, but they knew the group would be waiting, and they had no good excuse for backing out.

In the shower, steam swirled around them as Jabari leaned into Simone's touch, his eyes closed, smiling as her fingers gently lathered his hair and traced soft circles across his back. Her touch excited him and they fell back into bed.

Afterward, Jabari lay on his side, his arms draped around Simone. Her warmth pressed against him, her back fit perfectly against his chest, her hips pressed close to his, their legs intertwined. He brushed his lips against her shoulder. "We better get going," he murmured.

Simone sighed, the sound low and reluctant. "Do we have to?"

"I promised Aleshanee," he said. "Don't want to break it."

"I know," she whispered, slipping from his arms and heading to the bathroom.

Jabari listened as the shower ran for a few minutes before she returned and pulled on her clothes. Together, they made their way downstairs to the lobby.

Simone stepped over to Danielle, the inn clerk. "We're taking a hike to Paint Rock. My car is at Frazier and Sons, so if Mr. Frazier calls about my car, please tell him I should be back around three o'clock."

"Sure, darling. Have fun," Danielle said.

They stepped out of the inn and made their way back to Bridge Street, where the group stood waiting.

Aleshanee smiled radiantly and waved. "Good morning." She held out her arms inviting Simone in for a hug. The two women embraced and Alashanee turned to Jabari and wrapped her arms around him. "Thank you for taking us. I'm so excited."

"Glad to do it," Jabari said.

They marched over the bridge and turned onto the trail leading to Paint Rock. On the trail, cicadas burst into a chorus from the east, and another group of cicadas burst into song from the west. They went on answering each other in a glorious symphony.

"It looks like a storm is brewing," Dan said.

"Yes, but moving away from us. I think we'll be okay," Jabari said, and began whistling a tune as the group made their way along the winding trail.

"What's that you're whistling?" Dan asked.

"'Back to Nature' by Roy Hummings—a jazz tune," Jabari replied.

"You like jazz?" Dan asked.

"I like everything, really, but I love jazz most of all," Jabari answered.

"It's not my cup of tea," Dan said.

"To each his own," Jabari said.

On the side of the trail was a family of deer grazing in a meadow. When the group stopped to observe, they spooked the deer, and they ran away. The open space was covered in wildflowers—a rainbow of colors bursting up from the earth—swaying gently in the breeze. Starla stepped into the meadow, picking a few of the blossoms before trotting to catch up.

Jabari saw Starla quietly sidle up to Simone and lean in close to whisper something, throwing a quick glance in Jabari's direction. He couldn't hear what was said, but he caught Simone's smile—and the way her cheeks flushed a little. Her eyes flicked toward him, then back to Starla, and the two women burst into soft laughter, shared like a secret between friends.

"I hope this doesn't slow you down too much. You've still got a long way ahead," Simone said to Starla.

Starla smiled faintly. "Oh no, I'm glad to see it. But we can't afford too many detours."

Simone tilted her head. "What made you decide to hike the whole trail in one go, anyway?"

A look of melancholy came over Starla's face. "My mom did it all in one trip when she was young, and we had plans to do it together someday. Unfortunately, she fell ill," Starla explained, her head lowering. "Hiking the trail was important to her, but with her heart condition, she won't be able to do it again, I'm afraid. So, I'm doing it for her—also for myself—but mostly for her."

"I'm truly sorry to hear that," Simone responded with compassion.

Starla nodded, her lips pressed together.

As the winding path before them led upward, enticing them to higher elevations, the bustling town of Hot Springs gradually diminished in the distance. Simone eyed the flowing river below, her gaze then turning to Jabari, radiating genuine fondness. A memory of the night he and Simone had spent together by the river filled Jabari's mind, and he gently took her hand. Together, they ambled silently, savoring the serenity of the natural landscape.

Meanwhile, Starla continued ahead, seemingly preoccupied with her thoughts, while Dan followed behind.

The scent of smoke reached Jabari's nostrils, prompting him to search for its source.

Simone also noticed the smell, asking, "Does anyone else smell smoke?"

Jabari responded, "Yes, I do. Hopefully, it's just from a campfire." But worry began to gnaw at him.

A sign pointed toward their destination, indicating a path leading to Paint Rock. The path wound its way upward, bending gracefully toward Paint Rock. "I believe that's it. It should be just around the curve," Jabari remarked.

They reached the base of Paint Rock, a majestic formation towering over 100 feet above them. Jabari looked up at the ancient pictographs adorning the rock face, recalling Simone mentioning her fear of heights. He turned to Simone, saying with a hint of amusement, "The only way to get a good look at those murals is to climb the wall."

Simone quipped back, "Well, they won't be getting seen by me today."

Jabari laughed, taking the lead as they began ascending the narrow path, snaking along the edge of the rock formation, stretching upward toward its peak. The natural stairway created by tree roots and stones made the initial climb relatively easy, but as they climbed higher, the difficulty increased.

Gradually, the first remnants of murals, over five thousand years old, came into view. Alongside these ancient artworks were several displays of spray-painted graffiti. Various names and symbols covered the stones, and one particular eyesore caught their attention—a green heart with the words "Rob and Betty were here," defacing the sacred site.

"People have no fucking respect," Aleshanee seethed, her words punctuated by gritted teeth.

Simone placed a hand on Aleshanee's shoulder. "I'm sorry. People are assholes."

"You don't have to tell me," Aleshanee sneered.

They pressed on, following Jabari's lead, as they continued their hike along the path. Jabari encountered a sizable rock, rising to his waist in height. He effortlessly leaped onto it and extended a hand to Simone, who eagerly accepted his help. With Jabari's assistance, she made her way up onto the rock.

Aleshanee followed suit, grateful for the helping hand. "Thank you."

"My pleasure," Jabari replied, warmly. He reached down to lend a hand to Starla, but she was determined to do it on her own. Declining his assistance, she grasped onto a sturdy tree branch, leveraging her strength to reach the top of the large stone.

Evan nimbly hopped onto the rock, leaving Dan as the last one behind.

Dan struggled to find a foothold and stumbled on his initial attempt to climb the rock. Undeterred, he tried again, this time using a tree branch to pull himself up successfully.

The path grew narrower as they advanced, curving sharply over a cliff, exposing a perilous 75-foot drop onto a bed of rocks below. The treacherous terrain weighed heavily on Simone's nerves, causing her confidence to waver. She peered over the edge, her resolve waning, and she clutched onto a small tree, shutting her eyes to regain composure.

Jabari, taking note of her distress, called out from behind, "You okay, Simone?"

"No, dammit," she yelled.

"Should we turn back?" Jabari was concerned about her well-being.

"No, I'll be okay," she reassured him, determination in her voice. Slowly and cautiously, she maneuvered around the sharp turn, squeezing herself between the rocks and a small tree for support. As the path leveled off, she found solace against the rocky wall.

Aleshanee, displaying her agility, skillfully made her way around the cliff and stood alongside Simone.

Jabari effortlessly followed suit. "How are you feeling?" Jabari inquired, checking on Simone.

"I'm good, let's keep moving," she replied, with newfound confidence.

As they continued, the group encountered more Native American murals adorning massive stones.

Aleshanee seized the opportunity to document these ancient artworks using her phone, capturing both videos and photographs. Unfortunately, alongside the ancient murals, they also found graffiti spray-painted on the walls. The initials "SAS" were carelessly sprawled over one of the ancient murals. Aleshanee recorded the graffiti, expressing her disdain, "Whoever you are, SAS, you're an asshole."

Undeterred by the graffiti, they pressed on, ascending higher until they reached a breathtaking lookout point. From this vantage, hundreds of feet above the valley, they gazed down at the majestic French Broad River below, which meandered through the landscape. The view stretched for miles, showcasing the vastness of the mountainous terrain that lay before their eyes. Aleshanee stood boldly at the edge of the cliff, her long black hair gracefully swaying in the wind. The dreamcatcher tattooed on her arm seemed to come alive, gleaming in the golden sunlight.

Giving her space, Jabari and Simone stood back, understanding the significance of the moment as Aleshanee silently whispered a prayer to her ancestors.

Meanwhile, Evan sat quietly nearby, playfully dangling his feet over the cliff's edge.

As Starla and Dan joined the group, Dan couldn't help but marvel at the breathtaking view before him. "So, this is it," he said, in awe.

"We have arrived," Jabari confirmed, sharing the excitement of the moment.

Jabari moved closer to Aleshanee, both drawn to the awe-inspiring sight. Across the valley, they noticed another set of magnificent rock formations adorned with ancient murals that towered high above the French Broad River and Paint Rock Creek.

Pointing across the valley, Jabari observed more murals. "Those don't appear to be tarnished with graffiti."

Aleshanee responded, "That's only because the vandals can't get to them."

Jabari agreed, "You're right. I wish we could explore those caves and see what lies within."

Aleshanee nodded, her smile expressing a sense of wonder. "That would be amazing. And Jabari, thanks for bringing us here. This place is really special, and your gesture means a lot to me."

"It brings me great joy," Jabari remarked, and then caught another whiff of smoke. *Who is burning a campfire up here?* he thought. He ascended to a higher vantage point and scanned the surroundings to locate the source of the smoke. As he gazed across the Tennessee border, he spotted a colossal forest fire rapidly approaching their location.

Simone noticed the despair in his expression and followed his gaze, and then letting out a loud scream.

Starla looked and screamed, too.

"It's headed in our direction. We'll be cornered," Simone warned.

Jabari swiftly assessed their choices. Going back to the trail, they may be trapped by the fire, but staying on the cliff could expose them to suffocating smoke or even push them over the edge. "We need to get away from this cliff, right now," Jabari declared. He clasped Simone's hand, and together they hurriedly retraced their steps down the path.

Chapter Eight

Jabari and Simone rushed down to the edge of the cliff.

"We have to go, right now!" Jabari shouted.

Aleshanee spun around, bewildered. "What's happening?"

"There's a forest fire. We'll be trapped," Jabari explained.

Evan leaped to his feet and rushed over to see. "Holy shit! Run!" he yelled.

They swiftly navigated along the path, hugging the rocky wall as they moved, mindful of the treacherous drop beneath them. The path narrowed, leading to a sharp turn.

Simone avoided looking down and clutched a small tree, gracefully turning the curve like a cat. As the trail leveled off, she picked up her pace.

Jabari followed closely, maneuvering around trees and descending the natural staircase with long strides.

Each of them ran down the path toward the trail, trying to reach the trail before the fire did, and heading back toward town.

Jabari thought if they could make it to the river, they would have a chance. As they descended the rocky path, the smoke grew thick, and the air was murky. It filled their lungs and clogged their throats.

"I can't see," Simone said, "My eyes are burning."

Jabari held onto her hand, and guided her down the path. "Stay low," he instructed.

Dan coughed and gagged, looking as though he could lose consciousness at any time.

At that moment, the forest seemed quiet and still, with only the sound of crackling wood. The animals were long gone.

Jabari and Simone made it down to the trail. To their dismay, they saw that the fire was less than 100 yards away. Jabari looked for the rest of the group and was relieved to see Evan and Aleshanee stumbling through the smoke. *But where were Dan and Starla?*

Jabari sent Simone, Evan and Aleshanee ahead. "Get to the water," he yelled out.

Jabari waited for Dan and Starla. Peering up the hill, he saw nothing but thick plumes of black smoke towering upwards. He started back to find them, growing evermore fearful of what may have happened. *Did they fall?* Around a curve, he saw Starla struggling to help Dan down the path. He ran up to meet them. He wrapped his arm around Dan's side, as Starla did the same, the two helping him down.

On the trail, the fire was closer. Fueled by the wind, it was moving at a remarkable pace, and the sweltering heat scorched their skin.

Up ahead, Simone stood coughing and looking back for Jabari, Dan, and Starla—one hand on her hip and the other on her heart.

Seeing her, Jabari waved her ahead. "Go," he yelled.

Simone turned and continued running.

Dan leaned forward with his hands on his knees, trying to catch his breath.

"Are you okay, buddy?" Jabari said, anxiously, "We gotta go."

Jabari watched Starla grab Dan's arm, pulling him forward. He and Starla ran as fast as they could without leaving Dan behind. Jabari knew the river was at least a mile up ahead. The trees swayed in the wind, with the fire now moving alongside of them, and an unlucky possum lay burning in their path. Jabari leaped over it and continued. The heat turned their sweat into vapor.

The burning animal corpse seemed to motivate Dan to move faster. Eventually, he fell to his knees and threw up until he appeared to have nothing left.

Jabari saw Starla struggling to pull him up, but he wouldn't move. Again, Jabari stopped and came back to assist them.

Starla spoke in Dan's ear, "If you don't get moving, you're gonna get us both killed," she screamed.

Jabari grabbed Dan under his arm and hoisted him to his feet. He placed his hand on Dan's back and propelled him forward. "Just keep moving your feet, buddy. Don't give up," he said, knowing their chances of making it out alive were growing dimmer with each fettered step. Jabari looked at Starla and saw the worry in her eyes. Orange embers littered the air, falling like rain. The fire was jumping to the other side of the trail. Soon, it would surround them.

Up ahead, Jabari heard Simone screaming at them to hurry. Her voice cut through the smoke like a thread he could still follow. He squinted through the haze and caught sight of her. Flashes of their time together back at the inn and out near the river filled his mind. He yelled to Simone, "Go." He pointed. "Get to the river," he said.

Simone shook her head and directed Evan and Aleshanee

toward the water, which flowed about 200 yards from the trail. They ran toward it, weaving through trees and thick bushes. The forest grew denser near the river. Thorns ripped through their arms and legs. Simone looked back and saw that Jabari, Starla, and Dan were not far behind, but she didn't see the low-hanging tree branch which knocked her to the ground. She lay on her back, disoriented. Finally, she struggled onto her knees.

Jabari let go of Dan and ran to Simone. He dropped to his knees beside her, pulled her up, and steadied her as she found her footing and wiped the warm blood running down her face. "Are you okay?" he muttered.

The fire cracked all around them, heat biting into their skin, but he didn't let go of her. They had to keep going. There wasn't any other choice.

Jabari kept his hand wrapped around hers, anchoring her, as Simone stumbled forward. Finally, she looked at him and said, "I'm okay." He didn't believe her entirely, so he kept her hand firmly in his.

The group reached the gorge and climbed downhill to the river. When Dan lost his footing and tumbled down the hill, rolling into the water, ironically, it made him first to reach it. The group hurried down to join him, with the fire now racing toward them like a tidal wave. The forest burned along the ground and high up in the trees, red-hot embers falling all around them.

Jabari held tightly to Simone's hand, and together, they ran and jumped into the water. All six were now in the water but still not safe. The fire raged all around them, and the water grew uncomfortably warm. They were fully submerged in the water, only coming up for air, while Jabari held onto Simone's hand, refusing to let her go.

Aleshanee was far too exhausted to battle the deep currents. She could no longer hold her breath under water, so she floated on her back. A red-hot ember landed on her chest and burned through her shirt. She screamed and sank under the currents before Evan grabbed her and held her up.

Dan struggled to battle the current but held onto a fallen tree. He called out to Aleshanee, "Over here, Aleshanee. Come over here."

Aleshanee, finding new strength, swam to him and grabbed a hold of the tree.

The flying embers ignited the other side of the river. The fire blazed on both sides, the heat growing unbearable. If the water grew any hotter, it would boil them alive.

Simone wrapped her arms around Jabari and squeezed hard. Her embrace and the look in her eyes told him she was depending on him.

"Hold on, we're gonna make it," he said, just before she started to cry.

Eventually, the blaze moved beyond the river and raced toward town.

After sunset, the sky glowed bright orange for as far as Jabari could see. He kept the group near the water as they waited to be rescued. The worst of the fire had passed, but he knew they could still be in danger and needed to stay near the river until sunrise. As the temperature dropped, they had to worry about hypothermia, because of their wet clothes.

"I hope someone is coming to get us soon," Aleshanee said, shivering.

"I told Danielle where we were headed, but I doubt if they'll send a search party tonight," Simone replied.

"It's going to get cold overnight," Starla said.

Jabari thought for a moment. "In order to get as warm as possible, we need to remove these wet clothes. Everybody, take off your clothes and move in close together."

At his direction, they stripped down to their underwear.

They hung their wet clothes on burnt tree branches and huddled close together to keep warm.

Aleshanee sat fiddling with her water damaged phone, the screen smudged and blurry.

"I hope your photos survived, Aleshanee," Simone said.

"That would require a good measure of luck, which I clearly don't have," Aleshanee said.

When tears filled Dan's eyes, he wiped them away and swallowed hard. He had never come so close to death, and what a horrible death it would have been. He let out a sigh of relief when Starla rested her head on his shoulder and rubbed his back.

Starla sat shivering. "I'm so cold."

They needed a campfire, but there was nothing left to burn. They could only rely on each other's body heat to keep warm.

One by one, huddled up, they eventually fell asleep. But Jabari stayed awake. He hadn't felt this traumatized since the war. His mind raced, and his heart pounded in his chest. Once the plumes of smoke cleared, a full moon illuminated the charred landscape. He gazed at the stars and listened to the river. Afraid of what the morning would bring, the running water calmed his nerves, clearing his mind so he could focus on his breathing. He continued in this meditative state until sleep took him away.

Chapter Nine

The stars grew dim as the sun began its journey across the sky. Jabari pulled his damp clothes off the limb and dressed himself. He stood near the water, skipping rocks. He tossed each rock, using a sidearm motion, spinning rocks off his index finger. He released and counted each skip, one, two. He tossed again, one, two, three. He tossed again, one, two. He lowered himself to the surface of the water, and tossed again, one, two, three, four.

"Is that the best you can do?" Dan asked Jabari.

"You think you could do any better?" Jabari asked.

Dan picked up a rock and tossed, one, two.

"I didn't think so," Jabari mused.

"Hold on, that's only my first toss." Dan grinned.

Jabari crossed his arms and watched.

Dan found a flat rock and tossed again, one, two, three.

Jabari tossed, one, two, three.

Dan tossed, one, two, three.

Jabari tossed, one, two, three, four, and then turned to Dan and winked.

"Don't get too excited." Dan picked up another rock, kissed it, and held it to the sky. He tossed, one, two, three, four, five. He then crossed his arms and smiled, admiring his work.

Not wanting to be outdone, Jabari picked up a rock, kissed it and tossed, one, two, three.

Dan laughed and patted Jabari on his back. "Surrender, buddy. I never lose at this game."

Jabari frowned, not understanding why the loss bothered him so.

"In all seriousness, thanks for everything you did yesterday." Dan, this time, patted him on the shoulder. "I probably wouldn't be here if it weren't for you. Which is why I feel so terrible about whipping your ass just now."

Jabari laughed. "Don't mention it, buddy. But you should be thanking Starla."

They both peered at Starla who was sitting up and talking to Simone.

"Don't worry, I will," Dan reassured.

"Smart man. We should probably be getting back to town," Jabari said.

"Should we just wait for a search party?" Dan mused.

"I'm not completely sure there is one," Jabari said.

"Good morning," Aleshanee interrupted.

"Is everybody okay?" Jabari asked.

"I think so," Simone said.

"It is so cold," Aleshanee said, shivering.

"You should warm up a bit once we get moving," Jabari said.

The group collected their damp clothes and dressed.

Simone dipped her face into the cool river waters while Jabari carefully examined the cut on her forehead. "It doesn't look too bad, it's barely noticeable. You're still as beautiful as ever," he reassured her.

"It hurts like hell, though," Simone winced, trying to tough it out.

After gathering their strength, they ascended the hill, only to find that the trail seemed much farther than they remembered. As they finally made their way back onto the path, they were confronted with a harrowing sight—the forest lay devastated before them.

Starla couldn't hold back her tears as she gazed around. The once vibrant and teeming woodland had been reduced to a desolate expanse of torched earth and smoldering trees, and the once lively symphony of nature had fallen eerily silent.

As they traveled to higher elevation, the air was heavy with the scent of charred earth, invading their senses and causing tears to well up in their eyes. The group stumbled through the devastated landscape, their hearts heavy with grief, yet grateful for their miraculous escape. The meadow they gazed upon, once adorned with vibrant wildflowers, now lay in ruins, the once-lush field reduced to blackened remnants with burnt roots.

Taking solace in their decision to seek refuge in the river, they knew it had saved their lives. Simone, her eyes brimming with tears, covered her mouth in shock and sorrow. Jabari gently held her hand, providing a guiding presence through the desolation.

Upon returning to town, they found a cluster of firefighters and policemen huddled around a map, the flashing lights of emergency vehicles serving as beacons of hope.

Danielle stood near a firetruck, her hand resting on her hip, intently surveying the burnt forest. "There they are," she announced, as she spotted Simone and Jabari emerging from the devastation.

Relief washed over the firefighters' faces as they approached the missing group of hikers. Danielle rushed to embrace Simone and Jabari; her voice choked with emotion, "I'm so glad to see you guys. I thought you were dead, for sure," she confessed.

"So did we," Jabari admitted, his voice carrying the weight of their harrowing ordeal.

"They were getting ready to go in after you," Danielle said.

The firemen covered them with blankets, escorting them to an ambulance where they received first aid and hot chocolate.

Journalists shouted questions at them, and despite Jabari's efforts to deflect any undue attention, he was dismayed when he saw the narrative building around him. He foresaw the possible headlines: Police Officer Involved in Shooting Guides Group to Safety.

"We need to get you to the hospital," the paramedic urged.

"I'd rather not spend the whole day in the ER," Jabari replied. "I'll stop by Urgent Care when I get home."

Simone nodded in agreement.

Danielle helped them into a white fifteen-passenger van and drove them back to the Oak Tree Inn. On the way, she phoned her staff, asking them to have breakfast ready by the time they arrived.

When they reached the inn, Danielle led them straight to the dining room, where a generous spread awaited—fluffy eggs, crisp bacon, golden pancakes and waffles, a colorful array of fresh fruit, and steaming mugs of coffee.

Although Simone had lost her appetite due to recent events, the rest of the group eagerly filled their plates with the mouthwatering offerings. Grateful for Danielle's efforts, Simone expressed her thanks before the hostess tried to slip away to the front desk.

However, Dan insisted, "No, please join us. You must be hungry, too."

Danielle smiled warmly, accepting the invitation. Seated at the table, she helped herself to breakfast and poured a cup of steaming coffee. She smiled and spoke kindly, "I'm sorry you all had such bad luck this weekend."

Simone replied with surprising positivity, "It wasn't all bad. I wouldn't change everything that happened."

Jabari couldn't help but smile, appreciating Simone's affectionate words.

"I don't know how you all made it out of there. If you'd only seen the aerial footage from the fire last night, you would know how lucky you all are." Stuffing a forkful of eggs into her mouth, Danielle asked, "How did you all survive it?"

They told her the tale from the beginning—the singing birds and the beautiful meadow, their experience at Paint Rock, and the awful fire bearing down upon them. They told her how they were trapped on that cliff, and how they barely made it into the river.

Danielle hung onto every word. "God is good."

"All the time," Simone replied.

Aleshanee rubbed the burn spot on her chest and grimaced.

"Did the medics have a look at that?" Jabari asked.

"Yeah, but it still hurts," Aleshanee said.

Simone yawned. "I need some sleep."

"Of course," Danielle said.

"Thank you for everything," Starla said to Danielle.

"I'm just glad you all are safe," Danielle said, as she left the room.

"I'm done with this trip. I just wanna go home," Starla announced.

"Is there a train or something around here?" Evan asked.

"The closest airport is in Asheville, which is about a forty-five-minute drive from here," Jabari said.

"I can drive you all to the airport once my car is ready. It will be a tight squeeze, but we can make it work," Simone offered.

"That would be great," Aleshanee said.

"Where are your things?" Simone asked.

"We left our backpacks at the campsite, if it's still there," Aleshanee answered.

"Okay. I'll come and get you as soon as my car is ready," Simone promised.

Jabari and Simone left the dining room and climbed the stairs. When Jabari unlocked the door, Simone stepped inside first. He followed her in and closed the door behind them. Jabari dropped to his knees, and lay face-down on the floor, exhausted.

Simone sat in a chair nearby. She placed her foot on his shoulder and shook him softly. "Come on babe, let's get in the shower," she said.

"Go ahead. I'm right behind you," he said, wearily.

Simone stood under the warm water, letting it run from her head to her feet.

Jabari joined her under the warm water, leaning against the wall and letting the water run on his head and down his back.

Simone lathered up soap on his shoulders, arms, back, and legs, as he closed his eyes and smiled. "I wonder if my car is ready. I need to get home," she said.

They stepped out of the shower and dried themselves.

"How's your head?" Jabari asked.

"It hurts a little, but I'm okay."

He ran his hand over her wet braids and smoothed them back. "I'm so glad I met you."

"I'm glad I met you, too." She wrapped her arms around him, pressing her lips hard against his.

Jabari pulled her in close and kissed her back, her warm tongue making his head swirl. When their towels fell to the floor, Jabari lifted her off the floor, wrapping her legs around his waist and carried her to the bed, lying on top of her.

83

Chapter Ten

Jabari and Simone lay in each other's arms in a deep sleep. The ringing phone pulled them awake.

Simone rolled over and reached for the hotel room phone, "Hello," she said, groggily.

Jabari sat up and rested on his elbow, watching as she spoke into the phone.

"Okay, thanks." She placed the receiver in the cradle, rolled over, and nestled into Jabari's embrace. She tucked her thigh between his legs as he wrapped his arms around her waist.

"Who was that?" Jabari murmured.

"Russell. He said my car is ready."

"We'd better get up and get going," he said.

"Would you like a ride back to your car?" she asked him. "You shouldn't walk back through that wasteland."

"Sure. I'd like that." Jabari held Simone close. He liked the way her skin felt against his.

They rested for a while before Simone sat up and yawned. She peered down at him and twisted her lips while deep in thought.

"What's wrong?" Jabari asked.

"Oh, nothing. I was thinking about your troubles back home and the ongoing trial. I wonder how your fellow officers will treat you after your testimony," she said.

"I don't anticipate any problems." Jabari rolled out of bed, slipped into a clean pair of shorts before stepping into the bathroom and brushing his teeth. He gathered his belongings and neatly packed them away.

Simone climbed out of bed and wrapped herself in a towel. "Let me freshen up right quick." She stepped into the bathroom and closed the door.

Jabari finished packing and stepped into his shoes. He sat by the window and waited for Simone. He also thought about the problems awaiting him back home, the civil unrest and his upcoming testimony.

Simone stepped out of the bathroom wearing a pair of leggings and a yellow t-shirt. Her braided hair was pulled into a ponytail. "All ready," she said.

They picked up their bags, exited the room, and descended the stairs into the lobby.

Downstairs, the lobby was bustling with guests who sat around watching the news and chatting about the fire.

"I'm hearing it was a lightning strike that started the fire," a man said to Jabari.

"You don't say," Jabari responded. He made his way to the front desk, where Danielle stood waiting.

"Checking out?" she asked.

"Yes, I am." Jabari handed over the room keys.

Danielle printed his receipt and handed it to him. "I hope you both enjoyed your stay, considering all that happened," she smiled.

"We did. Thank you."

"I take it your car is ready?" she asked Simone.

"Yes. We're going to pick it up now."

Danielle leaned over the desk. "There are some reporters out front," she whispered.

"Any way to avoid them?" Jabari asked.

"You can slip out back through the garden, and follow the path out to the road," Danielle suggested.

"Sounds like a plan."

Jabari picked up his backpack and he and Simone slipped out the back door and through the garden. They followed a path around the edge of the property, leading them to the road. They followed the road back to Frazier and Sons and stepped inside.

"Hi, Russell," Simone said.

"Hi there, Ms. Morton." Russell turned to the young man behind the desk. "Pull the Honda Accord around."

"What do I owe you?" Simone asked.

"That'll be seven hundred and eighty dollars," Russel said.

Simone handed Russell her debit card.

He swiped it through a machine and printed a receipt. "Sign here please."

Simone signed the receipt. "Thank you," she said.

"Glad to be of service. You get home safe, you hear," Russell said.

Jabari and Simone stepped outside where her car sat waiting. They placed their bags in the trunk and climbed inside.

Simone settled in behind the steering wheel and inserted her key into the ignition. She gritted her teeth, looked away, and gave it a try. The car started without incident. She was relieved. Simone drove to Bridge Street and looked around for the group.

"There they are," Jabari pointed.

Simone slowed to a stop and lowered the windows. "Hop on in," she called out. She popped open the trunk and stepped around to the back of the car. They stuffed in three of their four backpacks, but there was no room for Aleshanee's bag.

"I can hold it up front." Jabari took Aleshanee's backpack and climbed back into the front seat.

Dan, Aleshanee, and Evan were first to climb into the back. Lastly, Starla squeezed in and sat on Dan's lap.

"Is everyone comfy?" Simone asked.

"Oh, yeah," Starla said.

"I am taking Jabari to his car first, and then we'll go to Asheville," Simone informed.

"Sounds good," Aleshanee said.

They drove along the winding mountain roads. It seemed the blackened landscape would never end. They rode along in silence—taking in the devastation from the fire. They were relieved when the burnt landscaped ended and the forest turned green again. However, the smell of smoke was inescapable for miles. It had settled in their clothes, their hair, and in every inch of Simone's car.

They arrived in Davenport Gap and found Jabari's black Ford F-150 sitting where he had left it. He tossed his bag in the bed of the truck, and then texted Simone his phone number. Simone stood in front of him, stirring the gravel with her foot.

Jabari's eyes studied the contours of her face. "What's wrong?" he asked.

"I was just thinking about all that happened this weekend," she said.

"Yeah, it was pretty intense."

"I'm also wondering if we'll see each other when we get back?"

Jabari pulled her in close. "I want to see you *as soon as* you get back," he said.

Simone smiled.

After Jabari kissed her goodbye, Simone climbed back into her car and waved.

Jabari watched them drive away.

Chapter Eleven

Jabari climbed into his Ford F-150 and turned the key in the ignition. A Tribe Called Quest blasted from the speakers. Miles away from the fire, his truck reeked of smoke. He turned onto I-40 East and headed home to Durham. He wondered what awaited him in the Bull City, as the news of civil unrest weighed heavily on his mind. He worried for his brothers in blue, but he understood the community's frustration. He knew they had a right to be angry, and they had a right to protest, if it remained peaceful.

Jabari drove along Woodcroft Parkway, gripping the steering wheel until the veins in his arms swelled. He pulled into his driveway and looked around at his property. He almost expected to find the place vandalized, with graffiti across his front door. Instead, he found everything just as he had left it—calm and quiet. A sense of relief washed over him. He turned off the ignition and climbed out of the truck.

He noticed that the grass had grown in his absence, prompting a furrowed brow. He stepped up onto his front porch and saw the mailbox overflowing with lawyer advertisements, which had come in steadily since the release of the police video. He stepped inside and tossed them into the trash.

He swung open the refrigerator door and sifted through an assortment of craft beer, before grabbing a Harlem Sugar Hill Golden Ale. He stepped into the living room, kicked off his shoes in the middle of the floor, and plopped onto a tan leather sofa. He looked around his living room, realizing how much he had missed the place while he was away. After roughing it on the Appalachian Trail, the tan leather sofa made him feel as if he were sitting on a cloud. The couch came with a matching recliner. These pieces were mere components of a seven-piece living room ensemble, a recent acquisition that included a coffee table, twin side tables, and a pair of lamps. Mounted on the wall was a flat-screen television and a painting of seven Egyptian architects building the Great Pyramid of Giza. He turned on the television and took a swig of beer. His phone vibrated on the side table, the display bearing the name "Simone." A grin tugged at the corners of his mouth as he answered, "Hey, beautiful."

"Hey, Jabari. Have you made it home?" she asked.

"Yeah, not too long ago," he said.

"What are you doing?"

"Watching an old episode of *Martin*," he chuckled.

"That's good. I feel like you could use a laugh," she said.

"Ain't that the truth." He sipped his beer. "Where are you?"

"Passing through Greensboro. I'm getting some gas," she said.

"Do you want to get some dinner later on?" he asked, glancing at his watch.

"I don't think I can. I have work and a hair appointment in the morning," she said.

"You still have to eat, don't you?"

"That's true. Where do you want to go?" she asked.

"Saltbox Seafood Joint," he suggested.

"I'll call you later and let you know."

"Okay. Drive safely."

"I will. Bye."

When the call ended, Jabari settled back in his seat, crossing his legs. He thought about the long blades of grass growing outside. He knew the grass needed cutting, but he was too tired to move. His eyes grew heavy, as his mind drifted back to the night of the incident. He saw it all happen, as if reliving it in real time.

There he stood, staring down at Miles Goodwin's body. More police officers arrived on the scene and marked off the area with yellow crime scene tape. A sizable crowd of onlookers gathered nearby.

"Officer Miller," a voice called.

Jabari saw Captain Lucas approaching. "How are you feeling, buddy?" the captain asked.

"As well as expected," Jabari said.

"Can you tell me what happened?" Captain Lucas asked.

Jabari turned to face him, his hands and shirt covered in blood.

"On second thought, go to the trailer and get cleaned up first. I'll come see you shortly," Captain Lucas instructed.

"He needs to be covered up before his parents get here," Jabari told the captain.

"We will as soon as we can," the captain said.

Jabari nodded and stepped toward the trailer.

"The shooter," someone yelled.

Cellular phone lights lit up the street, as onlookers snapped pictures and recorded videos of Jabari passing by. A young woman wearing a black t-shirt with "Justice League" written in bold white letters across her chest, glared at him. A group stood around her wearing the same shirt.

Jabari turned away from her as an officer approached her.

"This is a crime scene. I need you guys to move across the street," he ordered.

"We just want to make sure y'all do right by that young man," the woman said, pointing to Miles Goodwin's body.

"You can do that from across the street," the officer said.

"We'll do it from right here," the woman responded.

Jabari stepped into the trailer and removed his bloody shirt.

Another officer entered behind him. "The woke mob is here ready to stir up some shit," he said.

"Yeah, I saw them," Jabari said.

"Are you good, brother? Do you need anything?" the officer asked.

"No, I'm good." Jabari washed his hands and face at the small sink. He slipped on a Durham PD jacket and buttoned it up. He stepped out of the trailer where the Police Chief and the Captain stood talking.

"There he is," someone yelled.

The woman wearing the Justice League t-shirt flipped her long braids over her shoulder and screamed, "What do we want?"

"Justice," the crowd responded.

"When do we want it?" she screamed.

"Now!"

"What do we want?"

"Justice."

"When do we want it?"

"Now!"

Police Chief Justina Mathews turned to Jabari. "Are you okay, Officer Miller?"

"Yes, ma'am," he answered.

She turned to Captain Lucas. "Get him to the station. You can take his statement there."

Jabari awoke to the *Martin* theme song as another episode started. He stood and downed his now-warm beer. He went out to the garage and pressed the button on the garage door opener. Sunlight illuminated the garage as the door rolled up onto the ceiling. He wondered if he should go back for his firearm but decided against it. He pushed the lawnmower out into the yard and removed the gas cap. He stepped back into the garage and grabbed a canister of gasoline, filled the mower, and tightened the gas cap.

He pulled the string on the lawnmower and fired it up. He pushed the mower in straight lines along the side of his house, before moving to the front yard, where he noticed a black car with tinted windows parked on the street in front of his house, its engine idling. When the passenger-side window started to lower, Jabari suddenly regretted leaving his firearm inside. A man sitting behind the steering wheel raised his cell phone and snapped a picture, before speeding off. Jabari sighed in relief before continuing.

He dumped the grass clippings into a clear plastic bag and left it on the side of the house. He used a weed eater to trim along the driveway and street, and then used a leaf blower to blow away the clippings. Upon finishing, Jabari surveyed his work. His lawn was thick, green, and lush. Compared to his neighbors' yards, he was satisfied he still had the best yard on the street. He put away his lawn equipment and went inside.

Jabari poured himself a glass of sweet tea from the fridge and headed out to the back porch. He sat and took a long swallow as he gazed at the sun dipping below the trees.

"You just can't seem to stay out of trouble, can you?" a voice said.

Jabari shifted his gaze and caught sight of his neighbor,

Germain Martin, making his way over from the adjoining property.

"Not lately." He reached out for a friendly hand slap that seamlessly transitioned into an interlocked finger clasp.

Jabari and Germain were college buddies and close friends, and Germain also happened to be Jabari's go-to real estate guru. Germain and his wife, Shanice, ran a successful real estate business, and on one evening of casual conversation, during one of Jabari's visits to Germain's abode, Jabari had let slip his fondness for their neighborhood. When Germain learned that his neighbor would be moving, he orchestrated a quiet agreement, allowing Jabari to lay claim to the home before it ever graced the public listings.

"What the hell happened?" Germain asked.

"It's a long story, my man. I'm just glad to be alive."

"Shanice and I were out to dinner last night, and guess whose face popped up on the news?" Germain said.

"I was afraid of that," Jabari said, as Germain sat next to him. "Beer?" Jabari asked.

"Sure," Germain answered.

Jabari stepped inside and grabbed a few beers from the fridge. He placed them in a cooler and went back out on the porch. He set the cooler between them. "Help yourself," he said.

Germain grabbed a bottle and popped off the top. "Have you been out today?" he asked Jabari.

"No man, I'm lying low," Jabari said.

"Yeah, it's been crazy out there. There's been protests almost every night," Germain said.

"Yes. I'm aware."

"I'd avoid going downtown for anything if I were you. By the way, did you get a chance to check out that property?" Germain asked.

"I did."

"Well, what did you think?"

"It needs a lot of work," Jabari said.

"It's a good price. Her father left it to her, and she just wants to get rid of it," Germain said.

"Yeah, I've been looking into that, and it turns out that he also owned the two properties next door."

"Yeah, but those aren't worth shit," Germain said.

"They just need a little work. Do you think she'll sell me all three for two hundred and fifty thousand dollars?" Jabari asked.

"That sounds reasonable, but what's your angle?" Germain asked.

Jabari leaned forward. "Listen, that entire section of Fayetteville Street will be completely changed in five years. They've already started gentrifying that area, and there is nothing we can do about it. So, I figure I'll buy all three properties, fix them up a bit, hold on to them for as long as I can, and when I eventually sell, I should stand to make a pretty good profit."

"That makes sense," Germain said.

"Will you draw up the offer?" Jabari said.

"I'll get on it right away. Besides, I'll make any excuse to see her again."

"So, she's fine, huh?" Jabari asked.

"You gotta see her to understand. But speaking of fine, who was that sister you were with on the news?"

"Simone—we just met on the Appalachian Trail." Jabari relaxed a bit. "You may meet her one of these days."

"Aww man, I knew it," Germain said, laughing. "Y'all seemed real comfortable with each other." He placed his hand on Jabari's shoulder and shook it.

Jabari laughed and settled back into his seat again. He heard several car doors slamming and loud voices coming from the front of his house. "What the hell?"

The two men hopped up and hurried around to the front of the house, where two dozen protesters gathered on the street chanting, "Tell the truth. Tell the truth!"

Some protesters held signs with Miles Goodwin's face on them.

"Get out of here," Germain yelled.

"Tell the truth. Tell the truth."

Germain turned to Jabari, shaking his head. "Local college students. Go on inside. I got this."

Jabari crossed his arms and stood watching.

"Get the fuck out of here," Germain yelled, waving his arms.

A young man approached Germain and faced him. "Look bro, we just want to make sure when he testifies this week, he says what really happened."

"He will," Germain said.

"How do you know that?" the protester asked.

"Because I know him. Besides, the video speaks for itself," Germain said.

"Just make sure he does right by Miles Goodwin," the young man said.

The group continued chanting, "Tell the truth. Tell the truth."

"Look, young man, he's a cop. If he calls this in, which would be his right to do, how long do you think it will take before the police got here? What do you think would happen to all of you? Do you want that smoke?" Germain asked.

The young man cut an eye at Jabari, who was watching and listening with folded arms. "Just make sure he does right by Miles Goodwin," the young man insisted.

"He will. Now leave him alone," Germain said.

The young man stared at Jabari for a moment before backing away. "Tell the truth. Tell the truth." The young man rejoined the group, before turning to face them. "Let's go," he yelled.

The protesters climbed back into several vans and SUVs and drove away.

Germain stepped over to Jabari. "Are you good, bro?"

"Yeah, I'm good," Jabari answered.

"Don't worry about that foolishness. This will all be over soon," Germain assured.

"That depends on the verdict."

"When do you testify?"

"On Thursday," Jabari answered.

Germain nodded.

"Look, I'll talk to you later, man," Jabari said. "I need some rest."

"All right, keep your head up, bro." Germain slapped five with Jabari and embraced him in a bro hug before stepping back over to the adjacent yard.

Jabari stepped into the house and flopped onto the couch, lay back and crossed his legs. *I don't need this shit. I should just focus on real estate for a living,* he thought. He turned on the television, flipping through channels before settling on baseball —The New York Yankees against the Boston Red Sox.

He lay there, partly watching the game, while stewing in his anger, when he heard a knock at the door. He stood, crossed the room and looked through the peephole seeing three of his buddies, off-duty officers, carrying a case of beer and a bottle of Jack Daniels. He pulled open the door. "Hey, fellas."

"Hey, brother. Heard you had some trouble today," Sergeant Maurice Cooper said.

"Just some college students. No big deal," Jabari said.

"They can be the worst ones," Adam Lee said.

Sergeant Cooper set the case of beer on the table and

ripped it open. He tossed a can to Jabari and took one for himself. "When did you get back?" he asked.

"This afternoon," Jabari answered.

"What the hell happened in Hot Springs? You were all over the news," Tom Clark asked.

"Long story," Jabari said.

"Give me the short version," Tom said.

Jabari sighed, growing tired of telling it, but he obliged with an abridged version of the tale. "I met a group of hikers on the trail, we were on our way to Paint Rock, a Native American heritage site nearby, and became trapped in the forest fire," he explained. He told him how they were nearly trapped on the cliff and described running through the forest with the fire blazing, barely making it to the river. "Soaking wet, we slept huddled together to keep warm before making it back to town as a search party was preparing to go in after us. That's the part you likely saw on the news," Jabari said.

"Haven't you seen it?" Sergeant Cooper asked.

"I lived it. I don't need to see it." Jabari said.

"That's a crazy fucking story, dude," Adam Lee said.

"You're one lucky son-of-a-bitch," Tom added.

"None of this is my idea of good luck," Jabari said.

"When do you testify?" Tom asked.

"On Thursday," Jabari said. "I'll be the last to testify, so hopefully this will all be over by the weekend, and I can get back to work." Jabari finished his beer.

Adam went into the kitchen and returned with four cocktail glasses. He turned his Boston Red Sox cap around backwards and opened the bottle of Jack Daniels. He poured double shots of whiskey into each glass.

They all downed the shots quickly, and Adam filled their glasses again.

"Isn't Smith testifying?" Tom asked.

"It wouldn't be in his best interest to testify," Sergeant Cooper said.

"Poor bastard," Adam offered.

"Him or Miles Goodwin?" Jabari asked.

"Smith is young and inexperienced," Adam said.

"Hotheaded is what he is," Jabari blurted out. "You can't tell him shit."

"He's not used to dealing with those people," Adam said.

Jabari held his full shot glass. "Do you mean *Black* people?"

Adam squinted his blue eyes. "He's from Utah, bro. He didn't grow up around any Black people."

"And that's an excuse?" Jabari challenged.

"No, but he probably got nervous," Adam said.

"Dude, you know you're sitting in my fucking house, right?" Jabari quipped.

"Come on, Jabari. Don't twist my words like that. Besides, I don't think of you as Black anyway. You're one of us," Adam said.

"That's not a fucking compliment," Jabari said, raising his voice. "I see your humanity, why can't you see mine?"

"Whoa, whoa," Sergeant Cooper interjected. "Adam, shut the fuck up, man," his gritted white teeth flashed under his mahogany-toned face.

Adam turned his red face toward the television and furrowed his brow.

Jabari went to the kitchen and tossed a pack of hotdogs and french fries into the oven. He opened a can of vegetarian baked beans, poured them into a pot, and set it on the stove.

Sergeant Cooper came in and leaned against the counter. "Don't mind Adam. I don't think he meant any harm. Just a little too much to drink."

"Don't bring that motherfucker back to my house," Jabari said.

"Now is not the time for us to be divided, bro," Sergeant Cooper warned. "We have to stand together."

Jabari grunted and looked away.

Sergeant Cooper leaned against the countertop and drank his beer. "Have you seen this?" Cooper pulled out his phone and opened a video, handing the phone to Jabari.

Jabari clicked play and saw the leader of the Justice League, an anti-police brutality group, standing on Mount Merrill in Durham Central Park, speaking into a microphone.

"I've been in this fight for a long time, but this particular fight hits home for me, because Miles Goodwin reminds me so much of my own cousin who was killed by police twelve years ago," she said, wiping her eyes. *"Corey Tucker died on May thirteenth, two thousand and ten. He was a freshman in college, home on spring break. He loved music, and he was simply walking home one night wearing headphones. I wish I knew what he was listening to, but we'll never know. As he was walking along, a police officer approached him from behind, pointing his weapon at Corey's back. Witnesses say the officer yelled commands at Corey, but Corey couldn't hear what the officer was saying. When he reached for his iPod to turn off the music, the officer shot him four times, killing him instantly. The police claimed it was a matter of mistaken identity, but they never gave him a chance to identify himself. They offered a half-hearted apology and moved on as if it had never happened at all.*

"Our family wanted justice, but there was none to be had, because no one cared about Corey. The chief of police didn't care, and neither did the mayor. They, in fact, lectured his family about how tough police work is, asking us to have empathy for what the officer and his family were going through. The district attorney didn't care, and neither did the grand jury, about what my family was going through when he said, 'It was a reasonable mistake'. The family reached out to the media; they didn't care

either. They, instead, reported that Corey had marijuana in his system—as if that meant he deserved to die—as if they hadn't used marijuana when they were in college—as if they don't use it now.

"Corey had done everything right. He had done everything we are told we need to do to be successful and to be accepted by society. The only thing he had ever done wrong was to be Black and live in a poor neighborhood, and he died because of it," she said.

"Make it plain, sister," someone yelled.

"Yet, they lecture us about how we must behave in order to avoid getting killed, as if we're the ones with extensive training. We know they have a tough job, but that is why everyone shouldn't be allowed to do it."

"That's right," someone else yelled out.

"Yet, even when the shooter isn't the police, even when the shooter is a security guard or a neighborhood watchman, they still don't face consequences. We still don't get justice. Why is that? Because our lives don't matter to them. But our lives matter to us. Corey's life mattered. Miles Goodwin's life mattered. That's why I got into this fight, and that's why we're here today, to make them care whether they want to or not! So, say his name!"

"Corey Tucker!"

"Say his name!"

"Corey Tucker!"

"Say his name!"

"Miles Goodwin!"

"Say his name!"

"Miles Goodwin!"

Jabari handed the phone back to Cooper and brought his fist down hard on the table. "This whole thing is just too much."

"It will all be over soon," Sergeant Cooper said.

"Not soon enough."

"I'm taking the boat out to do some fishing this weekend," Sergeant Cooper said.

"Oh, yeah?"

"Yeah, why don't you come out? It'll take your mind off all this shit."

"I'll let you know," Jabari said, with a raised eyebrow.

When the food was ready, Jabari and Sergeant Cooper fixed their plates and went back into the living room. "Help yourselves if you're hungry," Jabari offered Adam and Tom, as he sat down. He bit into a hotdog and focused on the baseball game. It was the bottom of the seventh inning, and the Yankees led by two.

Adam and Tom went into the kitchen and returned moments later holding plates of food.

"Thanks, man," Adam said.

"Welcome," Jabari mumbled.

When the game ended, the three officers stood and made their way to the door.

"You guys good to drive?" Jabari asked.

"Yeah, I'm good," Sergeant Cooper said, as he stepped outside. He turned and held up his fist. "Let me know if you need anything."

"Will do," Jabari said.

The two men fist bumped, and Jabari closed the door, stumbled into his bedroom, and lay across the bed.

Chapter Twelve

With a pounding headache and a queasy stomach, Jabari realized that the morning held no respite from the lingering effects of last night's indulgence. He reached for his phone and realized he had left it in the other room. He climbed out of bed and stepped into the living room where he found his phone sitting on the coffee table. He reached for it and saw two missed calls and two text messages from Simone.

"Ahh, dammit," he said, through gritted teeth.

The first text message read:

Hi Jabari, I was able to move some things around so we could have dinner, if you're still interested. I'll be ready in twenty minutes.

The second text message came an hour later:

Another time, I guess.

Jabari recalled inviting Simone to dinner. He shook his head, sat on the couch, and attempted to call her back. She didn't answer.

"Hi, it's Simone. I'm sorry I'm unavailable to take your call

at this time, but if you leave your name, number, and a brief message, I'll return your call as soon as possible."

"Hi Simone, it's Jabari. I'm sorry I missed you last night. Call me back when you can. Bye," he said, and ended the call. *I'm sure she thinks I'm an asshole,* he thought.

Jabari made his way to the bathroom and climbed into the shower. Standing under the hot water, he thought about delivering his upcoming testimony. He wondered what questions the opposing counsel would ask, and how he would answer. He squeezed body wash onto a washcloth and scrubbed his chestnut skin until a thick lather covered his body. As he showered, his mind wandered back to the night of the shooting. He replayed the entire day in his mind, timestamping every moment.

After showering, Jabari slipped into a pair of jeans and a gray t-shirt. He stepped into the kitchen and started the coffeemaker. He scrambled a few eggs, sliced some strawberries and a banana, and buttered some lightly toasted bread. He sat at the table and sent a text to Simone.

Good morning. What's your schedule today?

He saw three text bubbles appear, but he received no reply. He sighed and ate his meal.

Jabari spent the day at home. He cleaned up around the house, did his laundry, and watched a few movies. He turned on the evening news and saw the streets had remained quiet throughout the day, and he wondered what nightfall would bring. He picked up his phone and sent a text.

Jabari: Hi Simone. How was your day?

Simone: Busy.

Jabari: Okay. Talk later?

Simone: Sure.

Jabari smiled. *She's a tough one,* he thought.

Jabari: I had some trouble yesterday.

Simone: What sort of trouble?

Jabari: Some protesters showed up at my house. Then guys from work came over to check on me, and we drank too much. That's why I missed your call.

Moments later the phone rang. It was Simone. "What happened?" she asked, when he answered.

"No big deal. Just some NCCU students," he said.

"I'm sorry," she offered.

"It's cool. How was your day?" he asked.

"Long. I'm tired and I have class tomorrow," she said.

"What time?"

"Nine o'clock," she answered.

Jabari grunted.

"What's wrong?" she asked.

"Oh, nothing. I was hoping to see you is all," he said.

"Sorry..."

"I understand. I need to be ready for court tomorrow anyway," he said.

"That's right, you're testifying."

"Yes, I am."

Simone let out a loud breath. "On second thought. I'll be there in an hour," she said.

"Cool, I'll text you the address. Have you had anything to eat?" he asked.

"Not yet."

"I'll fix something," he said.

"Okay, I'll see you soon." Simone ended the call.

Jabari darted to the fridge and opened the freezer. He pulled out a package of chicken andouille sausages and placed it in the microwave oven to defrost. Meanwhile, he sliced an onion and a green pepper in half and chopped them into small pieces. He cut a zucchini into thin slices and rinsed some baby bella mushrooms under cold water. He poured avocado oil into a pan and set the temperature to medium and scraped the vegetables into the pan. As the veggies sautéed, he peeled and minced two cloves of garlic and added them to the pan.

Jabari filled a large pot with water and set the temperature to high heat. He pulled the chicken andouille sausages from the microwave and sliced them. He added the meat to the pan, mixing them into the sautéed veggies. He added salt, pepper, herbs, Italian seasoning, and a sprinkle of Ethiopian berbere seasoning. As the pot of water began to boil, he ripped open a box of spaghetti, pouring in the noodles, and set the timer for eleven minutes. He kept watch over the sautéing veggies, stirring them until lightly browned and softened, and then added a jar of marinara sauce to the pan. He stirred the sauce, mixing in the meat and veggies and watched until tiny red bubbles were rising to the top of the pan and bursting. He reduced the temperature and let it simmer, filling the house with an aroma of herbs and spices.

The doorbell sounded and Jabari hastened to the door and pulled it open. "Hi," he said, delighted to see Simone standing on his porch.

"Hi, Jabari," she said, smiling back at him.

Jabari looked her over and admired the pair of blue jeans and white halter top she wore. Her coiled curly hair hung at her shoulders. "You took down your braids," he said.

"Yes," she said, running her finger through her coiled curls. "I had to get the smoke out," she said.

"It looks nice," he said.

"Thanks." She smiled. "Are you going to let me in, or should I sit on the steps?"

Jabari laughed. "Come on in, silly." He stepped aside and held out his arms. When Simone stepped into his embrace, he squeezed her gently. The timer on the noodles sounded, he backed up and said, "Excuse me for a moment." He motioned for her to have a seat and rushed toward the kitchen. He poured the noodles into a strainer and set them aside.

Simone, instead, followed him into the kitchen. "Emm, it smells good. I didn't know you could cook," she said.

Jabari winked and flashed his pearly whites. "I can do a little something."

"Can I help with anything?" she asked.

"No, I got it. I just need to warm some bread," he said.

Simone eyed the kitchen table. "Are we eating here?" she asked.

"Yup."

"Where do you keep your plates?"

Jabari pointed to a cabinet door. "In there."

Simone moved across the room and pulled two dinner plates and two bread plates from the cabinet and placed them on the table. She found the silverware and set them beside the plates.

Jabari put four pieces of sourdough bread in the toaster oven. He pulled another bread plate from the cabinet and poured some olive oil into it. He added crushed black pepper, parmesan cheese, and basil pesto to the olive oil and brought everything over.

"What are we drinking?" Simone asked.

"Wine."

Simone pulled two wine glasses from the rack hanging on the wall and placed them next to the plates.

Jabari placed the bread on the table, and then uncorked a bottle of Cabernet Sauvignon before filling their glasses.

"Okay, let's eat," he said, and fixed their plates, and set them down.

Simone twirled spaghetti around her fork and pushed it into her mouth. "This is good."

Jabari's lips curled into a smile.

"Are you ready for tomorrow?" she asked.

"As ready as I can be—ready to get it over with, so I can get back to work." He coiled spaghetti onto a fork and pushed it into his mouth.

"How long has it been?"

"Five and a half months. I've been bored out of my mind," he said.

"I imagine so. What have you been doing, besides running from fires?" she asked.

"Not much of anything. I tried traveling to visit family and friends, but I get tired of either answering questions about the shooting, or for those who don't know about it, I pretend everything is normal. It's been better to travel alone, hence the hiking trip."

"I see," she said.

"What about you? How'd you spend your summer break?"

Simone sipped her wine and answered, "I taught summer school, so I didn't really have much of a break, but the fire certainly put things into prospective."

"How so?"

"Things I've been putting off, like experiencing Mardi Gras in New Orleans, or Carnival in Brazil, taking an African safari, or going to the World Cup. I think I'll make time to do those things now," she announced.

"Those all sound amazing. Maybe I'll join you," he said, with a hint of mirth.

"We'll see about your follow-through, sir." She beamed.

"Fair enough," he said.

Jabari swirled the wine around in his glass and drank it down. Flashbacks from the Oak Tree Inn filled his mind. He saw visions of him undressing her in the moonlight and running his hands over her smooth caramel skin. He gazed across the table, wanting nothing more than to taste every inch of her, and like before, he would take his time doing it.

Simone gazed back at him, as though she read his mind. She stood and collected the dishes from the table. "I'll take care of these." She placed the dishes in the sink and turned on the faucet.

Jabari crossed the room and stood behind her, resting his hands at her sides. He kissed her neck. "The dishes can wait," he said.

Simone turned and looked up at him, and let Jabari kiss her long and hard.

They moved into the bedroom, kissing and undressing each other slowly.

Lying on top of her, Jabari kissed her neck and her shoulders, before taking her caramel breast into his mouth. He kissed her stomach, her hips, and her thighs, and indulged himself in her alluring abyss.

Chapter Thirteen

Jabari reached for Simone as the sun peeked through the blinds. She wasn't there. He sat up and looked around. He pulled on a pair of shorts and a t-shirt and stepped into the bathroom, which felt warm from Simone's recent hot shower. Remnants of condensation were visible on the shower glass. He relieved himself, washed his hands, and brushed his teeth. He made his way to the kitchen, where he found Simone standing at the stove stirring a pot of grits and scrambling eggs. She wore his blue New York Yankees t-shirt, and her bare, toned legs cascaded down to the floor. Her coiled curly hair hung at her shoulders. "Good morning," he said.

"Good morning," she replied, smiling joyfully.

He kissed her on the cheek, poured himself a cup of coffee, and sat at the table, where toast, strawberries, sliced kiwi and honeydew awaited him. He saw the dishes from last night were all cleaned and put away.

Simone emptied the grits and scrambled eggs into two separate bowls and placed them on the table. "You have a big day ahead of you. You'll need your energy." She winked.

"You certainly tried to drain every bit of it out of me." He grinned devilishly.

"Oh, stop." Simone's dimples popped into view.

They both filled their plates and Simone eyed Jabari suspiciously as he added butter, salt, and pepper to his grits. She pressed her lips together and nodded.

"What?" Jabari asked.

"You passed."

"I didn't know I was being tested," he said, and raised his cup of coffee to his lips.

She pointed her fork at him and said, "You were and had you put any sugar on them grits, you would've failed."

Jabari laughed and almost spewed his coffee across the table. He wiped his mouth and said, "That's a northern thing, darling. I'm a southern gentleman," he placed his hand over his heart and nodded.

Simone eyed the clock on the microwave. "I better get a move on." She ate quickly and cleared the table.

Jabari remained seated and finished his coffee. "Thanks for breakfast. I'll take care of the dishes." He held out his hand and gestured for her to come to him. As she approached, he placed his hands on her waist and guided her onto his lap.

She sat on his thighs, straddling him, and wrapping her arms around his shoulders. "I have to get to work, and you have to get to court," she said.

"I know," he said, pitifully.

Simone smiled and brought her lips to his, as he ran his fingers through her coiled curls.

"Thanks for hanging out with me," he said.

"I had a good time," she said.

"Where's your place?" he asked.

"Downtown. I have a condo," she answered.

"Cool."

"I could try and make it to the courthouse after class if you want," she said.

"That would be nice," he nodded.

"Okay. I better get going." She stood and left the room.

Jabari cleaned the kitchen and poured another cup of coffee. He stepped into the living room and sat on the couch. The tan leather felt cold against his skin. He turned on the news and settled back in his seat. Soon after, he saw his face, along with Officer Smith's, plastered across the screen. A news reporter stood outside the courthouse and announced he was scheduled to testify. When Simone reappeared wearing a navy-blue pants suit, a red blouse, and red leather stilettos, Jabari stared at her as she approached. For a moment, he was unable to speak. He admired how her blue slacks hugged her curvy hips and full-moon derrière.

Simone leaned forward and planted her red lips onto his. "I'll see you in court," she said, and left the house.

"Okay," was all Jabari managed to say.

Jabari headed to his bedroom and quickly hopped into the shower. He dried his skin and stepped out onto white tile floors. He stood in the mirror, wearing a pair of boxer briefs and a white undershirt. He grabbed a pair of clippers from underneath the sink. Standing in the mirror, he trimmed the hair on his head and shaved the hair on his face he'd grown while hiking the trail.

He stepped into his bedroom and pulled one of his blue Durham Police Department uniforms from the closet. He removed the dry cleaner's plastic bag and laid the uniform across his bed. He pinned on his badge, several accommodation medals and various pins onto his uniform. He stepped back and looked it over, realizing he hadn't worn the uniform since the night of the shooting. He dressed and stood in the mirror, looking himself over. Satisfied, he stepped outside, climbed into his black Ford F-150 and headed downtown.

Jabari turned onto South Dillard Street and saw a sizable crowd outside the courthouse. Two police officers stood behind a road barrier blocking his path, so he stopped and lowered his window. "Hey, fellas," Jabari called out.

"Look who it is. How are you?" an officer said.

"As good as ever," Jabari said.

"Big day, huh?" the officer said.

"You could say that. How long has this been going on?" Jabari nodded his head toward the crowd.

"They've been out here all morning," the officer answered.

Jabari shook his head. "I'm trying to get into the parking deck," he said.

"No problem, come on through." The one officer gestured to the other to help move the barrier aside.

Jabari drove past them and pulled into the parking deck. He parked and climbed out of the truck, put his peaked hat on, and stepped out into the street and assessed the area. He proceeded to the courthouse. He weaved through the crowd and climbed the stairs in front of the Durham County Court House, where Civil Rights Attorney Elijah Moore stood with Miles Goodwin's family standing behind him. At the press conference, a group of reporters surrounded them yelling questions, and dozens of protesters stood across the street.

Jabari paused to listen.

"Miles Goodwin was a good student. His family and friends describe him as always having his nose in a book. He was curious about the world and curious about the inner workings of the human body. He had plans of going to college and studying biology, with a concentration in infectious disease. He enjoyed playing video games with his friends, staying up late nights playing games if his parents allowed it. He was a happy and cheerful young man, with a smile lighting up a room.

"Unfortunately, his life was not always cheerful, because his small frame and love of books often made him the target of bullies, as he was targeted during the last moments of his life. As a group of misguided teenagers attacked him, with every intention of beating him into oblivion, Miles defended himself as any one of you would. He stabbed one of his attackers in the leg, allowing him to get away. But he couldn't escape torment, because the biggest bully of all ended his life. He ended it from behind the shield of the Durham Police Department, and he has been hiding behind that shield ever since.

"The activists say we should defund the police. Others say we must reimagine and restructure the police, resembling the variety of staff functions in the Federal Prison System. I don't know what the answer is, but I know what we currently have is not it. Who can we call when we need help? I wish I had the option of calling someone who can see my humanity. I wish I had the option of calling someone who doesn't see my skin as a threat.

"Give me the option of calling a social worker or psychologist. Let me call someone whose first and only option doesn't involve a gun. That is the justice the Goodwins are asking for. That is the change they want to see," Elijah Moore said, his hand resting on the podium.

The protesters filled the streets, cheering.

"And as for Miles' family, who can never again revel in his infectious smile; for his parents who can no longer hug their son and protect him from the cruel world; what justice do they need? There is nothing that could make this right. There is nothing that could bring back their son. But holding officer Todd Smith accountable for Miles' murder would be a good start," Elijah Moore bellowed into the microphone.

Journalists shouted questions at the Goodwin family, but their questions were drowned out by the chanting protesters.

"No justice, no peace—defund the police. No justice, no peace—defund the police."

A vein in Jabari's neck pulsated as he passed by the crowd. He stepped inside the courthouse where there were two lines at the metal detectors. A sheriff deputy who stood by monitoring the lines, pointed to Jabari and waved him through. Jabari stepped past the metal detectors and made his way to the elevators. He rode the elevator to the eighth floor and found the District Attorney's Office. Stepping inside, he approached a young receptionist, a brown-eyed girl with short brown hair.

"Hi. I'm here to see Mr. Powell," he said.

"Yes, Mr. Miller, he's expecting you." She rose from behind her desk. "Right this way." She led Jabari into a nearby conference room. "You can have a seat—he'll be with you shortly."

Jabari sat at a light wooden table, taking in the quiet room. He spotted a coffee machine and moved across the room to look over the assortment of pods. He selected a flavor and started the brew. As the cup slowly filled, he tore open a packet of sugar, stirred it a few rotations, and snapped on a lid. He returned to the table with the coffee just as District Attorney Owen Powell entered the room clutching a red file to his side.

"Good morning, Mr. Miller," Powell said, extending a hand.

Jabari stood and shook it. "Good morning."

The two men sat across from each other.

"Thank you again for doing this. We truly appreciate it," Powell said, sharing a polite smile.

Jabari offered a faint nod. "How's the trial going?"

"As well as can be expected. But trying a police officer—it's never straightforward. Juries can be unpredictable." His smile faded as he opened the red file and scanned the pages. "All right. This will be fairly direct. As we discussed, I'll start with your background and then move into the events of the night of the shooting. That clear?"

"Yes," Jabari said.

"We'll walk through the timeline—from when you got the call, to your arrival on scene, the shooting itself, and everything afterward."

"Understood."

"And did you review your timeline like I asked?"

"I did."

"Now, once I'm done, the defense will likely cross-examine. We don't know which angle they'll take but stick to the facts and don't let them throw you off."

Jabari raised a hand to cut in. "I'll answer honestly. That's all that matters."

"Of course," Powell nodded. "Any questions for me?"

"No, sir."

The District Attorney checked his watch and stood, file in hand. "A security officer will be over soon to escort you to the waiting room. I'll see you in the courtroom," he said, reaching out once more.

They exchanged a firm handshake before Owen Powell turned and left the room.

Jabari stayed seated, slowly sipping his coffee. His gaze drifted to the window as his mind slipped back to the night of the shooting. The final moments of Miles Goodwin's life replayed in his memory—his heart quickened in his chest, and beads of sweat gathered on his brow. He wiped them away, closed his eyes, and drew in slow, measured breaths to steady himself.

The door swung open, and a security officer stepped in. "Mr. Miller?" the officer asked.

"Yes," Jabari replied with a nod.

"Right this way," the officer said.

Jabari drained the last of his coffee, tossed the empty cup into the trash, and followed the officer out of the office. They took the elevator down to the fifth floor and the officer led him through a door and down a short corridor to the witness waiting area.

"Here we are," the officer said, pushing open another door. "I'll come get you when you're called."

Jabari took a seat and tried to occupy his thoughts with something pleasant. Simone came to mind almost instantly. He could almost smell her perfume lingering in the air.

Before long, the door opened again. "You're up, Officer Miller," the security officer said.

Jabari rose and followed him into the courtroom and stepped up into the witness stand.

Chapter Fourteen

The gallery was packed with journalists and spectators. Jabari stared ahead, doing his best to avoid eye contact. Across the aisle, he saw the District Attorney's team reviewing notes and whispering quietly among themselves.

Officer Smith and his attorney sat at the defendant's table. When he crossed his fingers on the table and gazed at Jabari, Jabari looked away.

Jabari glanced at the twelve jurors to his right. The panel consisted of eight men and four women: four white men, three African American men, and one Hispanic man; two of the women were African American and two were White. A few of the jurors cast brief, curious glances in Jabari's direction.

The bailiff stood and faced him as the judge spoke, "Raise your right hand."

Jabari did as he was instructed.

"Do you swear or affirm under the penalty of perjury that the testimony you are about to give will be the truth and nothing but the truth?" the judge asked.

"I do," Jabari answered.

"Have a seat," the judge said.

Jabari sat facing the D.A. The courtroom door swung open, and he saw Simone slip inside and find a seat on the back row.

"Adjust the microphone so that it fits you comfortably," the judge instructed, "Then state your full name and spell each of your names."

Jabari did as he was told.

"Your witness," the judge said to the district attorney.

"Thank you, Your Honor. Corporal Miller, how are you doing today?" the D.A. asked.

"I'm well. Thank you," Jabari answered.

"Tell us where you work."

"Durham Police Department," Jabari said.

"And your rank is Corporal, obviously. Is that correct?" the D.A. asked.

"That is correct."

"What did you do before joining the police department?"

"I was a Sergeant in the U.S. Army."

"Did you serve oversees?"

"Yes."

"Where?"

"I did a tour in Afghanistan, in the Korangal Valley."

"Some call the Korangal Valley the deadliest place on Earth, is that right?"

"I've heard it referred to as such," Jabari said.

"Thank you for your service," the D.A. added.

Jabari simply nodded his head.

"What did you do after the Army?"

"I returned home to Durham. I grew up here, I went to school at NC State and earned a degree in Criminal Justice, and after graduation, I joined the Durham Police Department," Jabari said.

"Okay. Take us back to the night of the shooting. Where were you and what were you doing when you received the call?"

"It was about three hours into my shift. I was patrolling the Fayetteville Street and Roxboro Road area that night."

"You say you were three hours into your shift. What shift were you working?"

"Six P.M. to six A.M.," Jabari answered.

"Okay, where were you when you received the call?"

"Cruising Roxboro Road, near the Durham Freeway when I was dispatched to a stabbing on the corner of West Main Street and Corcoran, so I made my way there."

"Which route did you take to Main?"

"I sped along Roxboro Road and turned onto Main Street."

"Your Honor, the State would like to introduce exhibit thirty-five," The D.A. said, as his assistant placed a large map of downtown Durham on an easel. The D.A. pointed to a star on the map and asked, "Were you here?"

"Yes," Jabari answered.

He turned back to Jabari, "What time did you receive the call?"

"Approximately nine-fifteen P.M."

"So, when you set off toward the incident, was your siren on?"

"Yes, my lights and siren were on," Jabari said.

"Go on," the D.A. said.

"I sped along Main Street and slowed at the corner of Corcoran and looked for the suspect."

"Was he there?"

"No, he wasn't, but at that time I received another call from dispatch, saying the suspect was seen crossing West Chapel Hill Street, near the Marriott Hotel."

"Did you get a description?"

"He was said to be wearing a white t-shirt, covered in blood, and he was brandishing a knife," Jabari said.

"And what did you do next?"

"I proceeded along Corcoran, passed the Marriott, and proceeded along Foster Street."

"Why Foster Street?" the D.A. asked.

"Corcoran turns into Foster after crossing Chapel Hill," Jabari answered.

The D.A. stepped over to the map and examined it. "Yes, it does." He nodded. "Okay, go on."

"After passing the Marriott, I saw Mr. Goodwin cutting across the campus of the Carolina Theater," Jabari said.

"Was he running or walking?" the D.A. asked.

"Walking fast," Jabari explained.

"Okay, and then what happened?"

"I turned onto Morgan and proceeded to the theater. That's when I saw Mr. Goodwin turn onto West Morgan and head toward the Durham Arts Council. I called it in, and I pulled alongside him. When he crossed the street in front of my vehicle, I stopped and got out."

"What did you say to him, if anything?"

"I yelled, 'Police. Stop and drop the knife', but he continued on toward the Arts Counsel and Morris Street," Jabari explained.

"Wait a minute," the D.A. said, with a slight smile. "Morgan Street to Morris Street?"

"Yes," Jabari confirmed.

The D.A. turned toward the jury and smiled. "These street names are confusing, aren't they?"

"Yes, they can be," Jabari said.

The D.A. went to the map again and pointed. "Right along here?" he asked.

"Yes, that's right."

"Okay." The D.A. nodded. "What happened next?"

Jabari continued, "I pulled out my firearm and pointed it at him, as I trotted alongside him. I again ordered him to drop the knife. At that time, he stopped and backed up against the wall of the parking deck. I thought he was going to make a run for it through the parking deck, so I moved in closer and ordered him to keep still, and that's when I saw the bruises on his face and his bloody nose. I realized the blood on his shirt was most likely his own."

"Meaning what?"

"I could tell that he had been involved in an altercation, and I also realized he was only a teenage boy."

"And the parking deck is attached to the Durham Chamber of Commerce Building, correct?" the D.A. said.

"Yes, that's the one," Jabari confirmed.

"What else did you notice?"

"He looked scared and confused."

"What did you do next?"

"I holstered my firearm and pulled out my taser."

"Did you point your taser at him?"

"I did," Jabari answered.

"And what happened next?"

"I pleaded with him to drop the knife."

"You *pleaded*?"

"Yes."

"What did you say?"

"I said, 'Come on, son. Drop the knife, please'. He stared at me for a while, and I watched him loosening his grip on the knife. It eventually slipped from his hand and fell to the ground."

"What happened next?"

"I saw another squad car arrive and stop on the corner of Morris and Morgan. I kept my eyes and taser focused on the kid

—Goodwin, and a few seconds later, I heard a voice yell, 'Freeze'. Goodwin turned toward the voice in a bit of a jerking manner, and that's when I heard the gunshots." Jabari heard several spectators gasp at his recollection.

"Did you see where he was shot?"

"Several shots hit him in the upper torso."

"Meaning his chest area?" the D.A. clarified.

"Yes, that's right."

"What's the name of the officer who shot Miles?" the D.A. asked.

"Officer Todd Smith," Jabari answered.

"Do you see Todd Smith here today?" the D.A. asked.

"Yes," Jabari said, never taking his eyes off the D.A.

The D.A. turned and pointed to Todd Smith. "Is that the man who shot Miles?"

"Yes," Jabari said.

"Officer Miller, how soon did you hear the first shots after Mr. Smith arrived on the scene?"

"Maybe two or three seconds," Jabari said.

"How many times did Mr. Smith shoot Miles?"

"I heard eight shots," Jabari answered.

"All in the chest?"

"Yes."

"Why didn't you shoot Miles?" the D.A. asked.

"I didn't feel it was necessary," Jabari said.

"Didn't you feel threatened?"

"No, I didn't," Jabari answered.

"What did you feel, if anything?"

"Compassion. I just saw a kid who needed help," Jabari said.

The D.A. turned to the jury. "A kid who needed help," he repeated. "What did you do next?" he asked.

"I immediately ran over to the kid—Miles. I called for an ambulance and started CPR."

"What was Officer Smith doing at the time?"

"I'm not completely sure. He may have started securing the area," Jabari said.

"How long would you say you performed CPR on Miles?"

"Ten to fifteen minutes."

"When did you stop?"

"When EMS arrived," Jabari said.

"Going back, did you later learn what had happened to Miles before the shooting?"

"Yes."

"Please, tell us what you learned."

"Later on in the investigation, we obtained a video which showed Miles walking along East Parish Street, when a group of other teens attacked him, knocking him to the ground. The video shows them beating him. Then he produced a knife and stabbed one of his attackers in the leg. He stood and ran off," Jabari said.

"In your experience, would you consider that to be self-defense?"

"I would," Jabari answered.

"Your Honor, the State would like to introduce exhibit thirty-six, which is a video of the Miles Goodwin attack and his self-defense."

"Proceed," the judge said.

The D.A. pressed a button on the remote control, and a video started on a flat-screen television, mounted on the wall across from the jury.

The video showed Miles Goodwin walking along East Parish Street, in the last moments of his life.

The D.A. turned back to Jabari. "Officer Miller, can you identify the teenage boy in the white shirt?"

"That is Miles Goodwin," Jabari answered.

The video showed the group of teens surrounding Miles Goodwin as he stood near the statue of Major the Bull, and that group of teens punching and kicking Miles as he lay on the ground, covering himself. It also showed Miles pulling out a pocketknife and stabbing one of his attackers in the leg, just as Jabari described.

Miles Goodwin's mother was heard sobbing among the spectators.

The D.A. pulled a handkerchief from his pocket and wiped his eyes. He turned back to the judge. "Your Honor, the State would like to introduce exhibit thirty-seven, which is a compilation of the dashcam and bodycam footage from Officer Miller."

"Proceed," the judge ordered.

The D.A. turned back to the television and pressed a button on the remote control. The dashcam picked up where Jabari was driving along Main Street, approaching Corcoran, and proceeding on to the Carolina Theater, when Miles Goodwin came into view. The video switched to Jabari's bodycam footage when he got out of the car.

The courtroom spectators heard Jabari's voice ordering and pleading for Miles Goodwin to drop the knife. They watched the knife fall from Goodwin's hand, and they heard another officer's voice ordering Goodwin to drop the knife. They saw Goodwin turn toward the voice, and then the bullets ripping into the teenager's chest. Jabari's voice was heard once again yelling "Stop. What the fuck?" as he ran toward Miles Goodwin.

The D.A. paused the video and turned back to Jabari. "Officer Miller, you are heard on the video yelling 'stop' and excuse my French, but also yelling, 'what the fuck'. Who were you talking to, Officer Miller?"

"Officer Smith," Jabari answered.

"So, for the record, Officer Miller, you were yelling to the defendant, Todd Smith to stop shooting at Miles Goodwin?"

"Yes," Jabari answered.

"And pardon me, but when you were heard saying, *what the fuck*, were you saying that because you didn't understand why Todd Smith was shooting Goodwin?"

"Objection. Leading the witness," the defense attorney interjected.

"I'll allow it," the judge said.

"Go on, Officer Miller," the D.A. said.

"Yes, I wanted him to stop shooting. As I testified earlier, I didn't feel the boy was a threat," Jabari said.

The D.A. turned toward the jury, shook his head, and wiped his brow. He turned back to Jabari. "To summarize what you've told us today, Officer Miller, you received a call about a stabbing in downtown Durham. You proceeded to the location and pursued the suspect throughout downtown before getting out of your car and pointing your firearm at the suspect. Is that correct?"

"Yes," Jabari answered.

"And would you say that based on your military combat experience, and years of law-enforcement experience, you were able to assess the situation and determine that Miles was not a threat to your safety. Is that right?"

"Yes," Jabari agreed.

"And after making this assessment, you holstered your firearm and pulled out your taser, because again, you did not feel that your life was being threatened at the time. Is that correct?"

"That is correct," Jabari said.

"In fact, it is your testimony that you saw a scared teenager who needed your help. Is that correct?"

"Yes," Jabari said.

"In fact, it is your testimony that Miles Goodwin actually dropped the knife prior to Officer Smith shooting him. Is that correct?"

"Yes," Jabari said.

"And it is also your testimony that within seconds of Officer Smith's arrival, he shot Miles Goodwin eight times in his chest area. Is that correct?"

"Yes," Jabari said.

"And so, it is your testimony that within seconds of Officer Smith's arrival, and without any assessment or attempts at de-escalation, Officer Todd Smith executed Miles Goodwin?"

"Objection, Your Honor," the defense attorney stood and yelled.

"Sustained. Don't answer that, Officer Miller."

"Withdrawn, no further questions," the D.A. said, and took his seat.

"Your witness, counsel," the judge said.

Defense Attorney Langley stood and buttoned his suit jacket. He approached the witness stand and said, "Officer Miller, first I want to thank you for taking the time to testify for us today. I know it can't be easy for you," he said.

Jabari nodded.

"I only have a few questions for you, and I'll try not to hold you too long, okay?" he said, with his heavy southern drawl.

"I have as much time as you need," Jabari responded.

"Officer Miller, when you first received the call, what description did you receive for Mr. Goodwin?"

"I was told he was a black male, wearing a white, bloody shirt and holding a knife."

"And what were you told the suspect had done with that knife?"

"I was told that he had stabbed someone, but we did not have all of the details at the time," Jabari said.

Wade Langley turned toward the jury. "Do you know, Officer Miller, I have so much respect for what you officers do. I mean, you respond to an incident where a person had just stabbed someone, and is covered in blood, still holding the knife, and yet you bravely respond and attempt to apprehend the suspect. Sounds so dangerous. Are you ever afraid?"

"All the time," Jabari said.

"All the time," Wade Langley repeated. "And despite that fear, you respond anyway. It's so commendable."

"It's what we get paid to do," Jabari offered.

"Let's go back to when you were in your vehicle near the Carolina Theater. What did you see?"

"I saw Mr. Goodwin moving swiftly along Morgan Street, and when he crossed in front of my vehicle, I saw that he was still holding a knife," Jabari said.

"He was holding the knife, and you said you could see the blood on his white shirt? Is that correct?"

"Yes," Jabari answered.

"And that's when you exited your vehicle. Correct?"

"Yes, that's correct."

"Tell me Officer Miller, when you exited your vehicle, why did you draw your firearm?"

"Because at the time, I only knew that Mr. Goodwin was holding a knife that he had recently used to stab someone," Jabari said.

"Officer Miller, is it safe to say that you felt the suspect was armed and dangerous?"

"Yes," Jabari said.

"And when you initially pointed your firearm at him, is it safe to say you feared for your life at that time?"

"Yes," Jabari said.

And according to your testimony, Officer Miller, you say that your perception didn't change until the suspect was standing with his back against the wall and you moved in close enough to see the bruises on his face and his bloody nose. Is that right?"

"Yes."

"And, Officer Miller, is it reasonable to say that according to Officer Smith's perception, Miles Goodwin, who had recently stabbed someone, was still armed and dangerous. Is that reasonable?"

"I suppose it's reasonable," Jabari said.

The attorney turned to face the jury. "Yes, I imagine so. No further questions, Your Honor," he said, and returned to his seat.

Jabari gazed across the courtroom to Simone. Their eyes met, and a smile adorned Simone's lips.

"You may step down, Officer Miller," the judge instructed.

Jabari stepped down from the witness stand and moved across the room. He found a seat next to Simone and took her hand, settling back into his seat.

District Attorney Owen Powell stood facing the judge. "Your Honor, the State will recall Brittany Davis," he said.

A woman wearing navy blue cargo pants, and a blue Durham County EMS shirt entered the courtroom and made her way to the witness stand.

"I remind you; you are still under oath," the judge said to Brittany Davis.

"Yes, Your Honor," she replied, and took a seat in the witness stand.

"Mr. Powell," the judge said to the District Attorney.

The D.A. stood before the witness. "Good morning. I have a few follow-up questions for you about your testimony," he said.

"Okay," she responded, shifting in her seat.

"When we stopped yesterday, you were describing what you saw when you arrived on the scene. Will you take us back through that moment?" he said.

"Yes, as I said yesterday, when the call came in regarding the shooting, we were dispatched to the location. We arrived at the scene and parked the ambulance," she said.

"And what was the precise location?" the D.A. asked.

"West Morgan Street, near the Carolina Theater," she answered.

"What time did you arrive?" he asked.

"It was approximately nine-fifteen or so," she said.

"And what did you see when you arrived?"

"My partner slowed the ambulance to a stop, and I saw a police officer administering CPR to the victim," she recalled.

"Objection, Your Honor," the defense said. "She referred to him as the victim."

"Sustained, refer to Mr. Goodwin as the subject, Ms. Davis," the judge said.

"Yes, sir," she said.

"So, you saw an officer administering CPR to Mr. Goodwin. And then what happened?"

"My partner and I pulled our equipment from the ambulance and rushed over to the patient. I asked the officer to step aside, and we took over," she said.

The D.A. turned and pointed to Jabari. "Is that the officer you saw?" he asked.

"Yes," she said, then nodded.

All eyes shifted to Jabari, as he sat still and looked ahead.

"What happened next, Ms. Davis?"

"We assessed the patient and checked his vital functions."

"What were the extent of the injuries?" the D.A. asked.

"Multiple gunshot wounds to his chest," she said.

"Okay." The D.A. nodded and eyed the jury. "What happened next?"

"It immediately became clear that Mr. Goodwin was already deceased," she said.

"How did you determine Mr. Goodwin was dead?"

"He had lost a tremendous amount of blood, he wasn't breathing, he had no detectable pulse or heart rhythm, and his pupils were fully dilated," she said.

"Did you take him to the hospital?"

"No, sir. By that time multiple police officers had arrived, and they moved us aside and took control of the scene," she said.

"And what did you do after that?"

"We stood near the ambulance and waited until they were done," she said.

"Thank you for your time, Ms. Davis. No further questions," he said.

Defense Attorney Wade Langley stood and buttoned his suit jacket. He stepped toward the witness box. "I'm so sorry you had to experience all of this, Ms. Davis. It must have been a traumatic experience." His southern drawl was heavy.

"It's part of the job," she said.

"Yes, I imagine so. Tell me, Ms. Davis, was it Officer Smith who moved you aside?" he asked.

"No, sir," she said.

"Officer Miller?"

"No, sir. It was a supervisor," she said.

"How do you know it was a supervisor?"

"He wore a white shirt, and the other officers on the scene took directions from him."

He turned toward the spectators in the courtroom and asked the witness, "Is that officer here?"

"I don't see him," she said.

"I see." He shook his head, looking down at the floor. He raised his eyes to her and said, "Something is troubling me, Ms. Davis. I just can't get my head around why you didn't take Mr. Goodwin to the hospital. Can you explain it to us?" he said.

She sighed. "Like I said earlier, sir, by the time we arrived, it was clear that Mr. Goodwin was already deceased," she said.

The attorney turned toward the jury, pressed his lips, and rubbed his hand across the back of his neck. He turned back toward the witness. "Duke University Hospital was nearby, correct?" he asked.

"Yes, sir."

"How far away from Duke Hospital would you say you were, Ms. Davis?"

"I would say maybe nine or ten minutes," she answered.

He turned his gaze back toward the jury. "Duke University Hospital is one of the finest hospitals in the entire country, wouldn't you say Ms. Davis?"

"Yes, I would say so," she said.

He stepped over to the jury and leaned against the jury box. "Some of the finest doctors in the country work there, wouldn't you agree?"

"Objection, Your Honor, irrelevant," the D.A. called out.

"Sustained. Move on, Mr. Langley," the judge ordered.

"Yes, Your Honor," he said, with a raised hand. He turned back to the witness. "It just troubles me, Ms. Davis, that you wouldn't have rushed Mr. Goodwin to the finest hospital in the United States with some of the finest doctors. I mean, don't you think they could have revived him?" he asked, with a raised voice.

"I don't think so," she answered.

"Is that your professional opinion, Ms. Davis?"

"Yes, it is," she said.

"Are you one hundred percent certain they could not have done anything to help him? Anything that could have saved his life?" he said, loudly.

"I'm pretty certain," she said.

"You're *pretty certain*, but not one hundred percent certain, are you? You want to explain to his parents how you were *pretty certain*, when their child was dying in the street?" he shouted.

"Objection. Badgering the witness," the D.A. stood and shouted.

"Nothing further, Your Honor," the attorney said, and returned to his seat.

"Does the State have anything else for the witness?" the judge said to the D.A.

"No, Your Honor," the D.A. answered.

"You may step down, Ms. Davis," the judge said.

Brittany Davis left the witness stand and found a seat.

"Mr. Powell," the judge called out.

"The State rests, Your Honor," the D.A. responded.

"Mr. Langley," the judge said.

"The defense also rests, Your Honor."

Judge McAllister eyed the clock on the wall. We'll recess for one hour. Court will reconvene at one o'clock for closing arguments." The judge brought down the gavel. "Court is in recess."

As the courtroom cleared, Simone turned to Jabari, "I thought Smith was going to testify?"

"I guess not," Jabari said.

"Do you want to get coffee while we wait?" Simone asked.

"I don't need to hear the closing arguments. Let's get out of here." Jabari took her hand and stepped out of the courtroom and advanced to the elevator and waited. "Where's your car?" he asked.

"At home. I took an Uber," she said.

Jabari led Simone to a side door and circled around to the back side of the parking deck. He scoped the parking area for any journalists lying in wait as they approached his truck. He saw a man peering down at the street where a sizable crowd of spectators gathered.

"Journalist?" Simone asked.

"Could be." Jabari gripped Simone's hand. "Let's move."

They hastened to Jabari's truck and climbed inside.

"Made it." Simone smiled.

"We're not out of the woods yet." Jabari took a deep breath and turned the key in the ignition. The F-150 roared as the engine fired up.

The man turned toward the truck and trotted in their direction, and another man hopped out of a van holding a video camera.

Jabari hit the gas and darted from the parking spot. The tires screamed as he whipped the truck around the curve, down the ramp, to the street below. He approached the guard booth and slowed to a stop. He inserted the parking ticket into the meter while checking the rearview mirror. He saw the reporter running after him. The barrier gate lifted, and Jabari hit the gas, speeding out onto the street.

"My goodness, they're relentless," Simone said.

"Tell me about it." Jabari said, as the truck sped past the Durham Bulls Stadium, across the Durham Freeway, merging onto Roxboro Road.

Simone patted and rubbed his thigh. "We're good now, babe," she said.

Jabari slowed down and cruised the rest of the way.

They arrived at his house and ducked inside.

Jabari flopped down onto the couch. "I'm exhausted," he said.

Simone pulled off his patent leather shoes and placed his feet onto the ottoman. She sauntered into the kitchen and found what was left of the Cabernet Sauvignon they'd shared the night before. She emptied the bottle into two wine glasses and returned to the living room. She handed him a glass, kicked off her heels, and sat on the couch beside him.

He took a slow sip of his wine and eased back against a pillow.

Simone reached for the remote and turned on the news.

"Put on something funny," Jabari requested.

She flipped around until she saw Richard Pryor, smiling in a white tuxedo. She turned to Jabari with a smile. "*Harlem Nights?*"

"Perfect," he said.

"He was a beautiful man," she said.

"Can't argue with that."

"I would've loved to live in Harlem in the nineteen-twenties—the style, the jazz... it just feels like my time."

"Same here."

"Except for, you know..."

"...the racism," they said in unison, and laughed at their synchronicity.

Jabari drained the last of his wine and sank deeper into the cushions.

Simone took his empty glass and set it on the coffee table. She snuggled in close to him, resting her head on his chest, and watched the movie with him until Jabari closed his eyes and dozed off to sleep.

* * *

While reclining on the couch, Jabari stirred from his slumber at the sound of a ringing doorbell. Gradually, he sat upright and cast a curious glance around the room.

Simone rushed from the bedroom wearing Jabari's white bathrobe and a shower cap. She opened the door where a delivery man stood holding a pizza box and two smaller boxes sitting on top of it. Simone carried the food to the coffee table, opened the box, and looked over the veggie lovers pizza. Steam rose from the two boxes of barbecue wings and parmesan bread bites. Satisfied, she went back to the door and tipped the delivery man a $10 bill. "Thanks." She smiled and closed the door. She removed the shower cap from her head and sat on the couch.

Jabari stood and popped a parmesan bread bite into his mouth. "Be right back." He bounced into his bedroom, quickly removed his police uniform, and hung it in the closet. He pulled on a pair of gray sweatpants and a t-shirt and stepped back into the living room where Simone sat watching the evening news.

He proceeded to the kitchen. "Want a beer?" he called out.

"Sure," she said.

He pulled two bottles of Harlem Sugar Hill Golden Ale from the fridge and returned to the living room. He handed Simone a beer and sat beside her. Jabari filled his plate, before taking a massive bite into a slice of pizza and fixed his eyes on the news.

A reporter stood outside the Durham County Superior Court building and said, *"Jurors in the murder trial of Durham Police Officer Todd Smith are now deliberating after three weeks of testimony over the shooting of Miles Goodwin, an unarmed teenager. The City of Durham is on high alert for more civil unrest following this highly anticipated verdict. Standing by, I'm Victoria Aiden, ABC Channel Eleven Eyewitness News."*

Jabari sat back and took a swig of beer. "I don't see them returning with a verdict tonight," he said.

"Neither do I, but I have a bad feeling about this. The tension in the courtroom was so thick today, I could barely breathe," she said.

"I know. I felt it, too."

Chapter Fifteen

The alarm on Simone's phone sounded at six o'clock A.M. and Jabari awoke and ran his hand through Simone's hair. Her head rested on his chest, and her leg was bent across his thighs. "Wake up, babe," he said.

Simone rolled off him and turned off the alarm. Rising into a sitting position, she swung her legs over the edge of the bed and planted her feet on the floor. She then reached out for Jabari's discarded bathrobe that lay nearby. "Can you take me home?"

"Of course," he said.

She stood and pulled his bathrobe over her bare skin, made her way to the bathroom, closing the door behind her.

Jabari heard the shower turn on. He pulled on his sweatpants and t-shirt and slipped into the bathroom to brush his teeth. Afterwards, he made his way into the kitchen and brewed a pot of coffee. When it was done, he filled two coffee tumblers with the hot brew and twisted on the lids.

Simone soon appeared in the kitchen, barefoot and with her red stilettos dangling on two fingers.

Jabari handed her a cup of coffee and grabbed his keys. "Ready?"

"Let's be out," she said.

They strolled outside and Jabari helped her climb up into his truck. He closed the door behind her and stepped around to the driver's-side door. He settled himself behind the steering wheel, started the engine, and backed out onto the street.

"Where are we going?" Jabari asked.

"One-twelve Corcoran Street," she answered.

Jabari turned toward her and furrowed his brow. "Near the Bull?"

"Yes," she confirmed.

"But that's where..."

"I know," she said, cutting him off. "That's where Miles was first attacked."

"Why didn't you tell me?" he said.

"Does it matter?" she asked.

Jabari pressed his lips together and punched the gas. Passing through downtown, he found the city calm and quiet, and he hoped it would remain as such. Many of the downtown businesses were closed and boarded up. Protest graffiti covered the plywood and the walls. Miles Goodwin's face was everywhere, along with the quote made famous by his mother, "My son was a beautiful boy."

"Turn here," Simone instructed.

Jabari turned onto Corcoran Street.

"Right here," she pointed.

Jabari slowed to a stop in front of a sprawling complex of new condominiums. "How long have you been here?"

"A few months," she said, as she slipped her feet into her shoes.

Jabari climbed out of the truck and stepped around to the

passenger side. He pulled open the door and helped Simone step out onto the sidewalk.

She wrapped her arms around him and kissed him goodbye. "I'll call you after class."

"Okay, cool," he said, before climbing back into his truck. He gazed over at the statue of Major the Bull, where Miles Goodwin was first attacked. He sighed and drove away.

Jabari spent the morning running several errands. He had the oil changed and tires rotated on his truck, before buying groceries and returning home. He spent the day busying himself by paying bills and attempting to read. He couldn't concentrate much. Finally, he joined everyone else in the Bull City by turning on the news and awaiting the verdict.

* * *

Jabari's watch said 3:15 P.M. He reached for his phone and called Simone. "Hey. Did you make it home okay?" he asked.

"Yeah. It's quiet out," she said.

"That's good. Have you had anything to eat?" he asked.

"Not since this morning."

"Okay. I'll come by and get you," he said.

"I'm in apartment eight-forty-six. I'll buzz you up when you get here," she said.

"All right. I'm on the way," he said.

Jabari made his way downtown and turned in front of Simone's building. He pulled up to the gate of the parking deck, rolled down his window and typed 846 on the keypad.

"Yes," Simone's voice bellowed from the speaker.

"It's me," he said.

Moments later, the gate rolled up and Jabari pulled in. The parking deck was constructed in the interior of the building, and Jabari drove up to the second floor before stopping in front of a barrier arm. He received a text message from Simone with a security code, and when he typed it in, the barrier arm lifted. Jabari was able to drive along a series of tight curves all the way up to the fifth floor. He parked in a visitors parking space and stepped inside the elevator. He ascended to the 8th floor, where he found Simone's corner apartment and the door slightly ajar. Jabari knocked and pushed it open.

"Come on in," Simone called out.

Jabari entered the living space and looked around. The sparsely furnished apartment smelled of drywall and fresh paint.

Simone stepped out into a large open living space and invited him inside. The living space included the kitchen, dining area and living room with floor-to-ceiling windows, displaying a magnificent view of the city.

"Make yourself at home. I'm just finishing up some work." She sauntered back into her office and sat at her desk.

A large flat-screen television hung on the wall above a gas fireplace, where two porcelain red and white elephants stood facing each other on the mantel. The television was tuned to the local ABC News station.

Jabari stepped over to the window, let out a deep sigh, and gazed out at the city. From his vantage point, City Hall was to his right and the Lucky Strike Tower to his left.

Simone joined him in the living room and sat on the couch. She wore a pair of jeans and a maroon Hillman College t-shirt. "I have binoculars if you want?" she said.

"No, thanks."

She reached for the remote and turned up the volume on the television. "Still no verdict?"

"Not yet." Jabari moved over to the couch and sat beside her.

"Where are we going to eat?" she asked.

"Dame's?" he suggested.

"That'll work." She slipped her feet into a pair of maroon and gray Nike Air Force Ones and grabbed her purse. They strolled out to the parking deck, hopped into the truck, and descended to the street.

Jabari headed to Foster Street and circled the block looking for an open parking space. Finally, he stopped in front of Dame's Chicken and Waffles. "You can get out and wait for me while I park."

"No. I'll walk with you," she said.

"All right." He circled the block once more before finding a space one street over, near the entrance of Durham Central Park. He strolled, hand-in-hand with Simone, over to the restaurant and the two went inside. "Reservations for Miller, party of two."

The hostess confirmed his reservation and grabbed two menus from behind the podium. "Right this way," she said.

Jabari and Simone followed the hostess to their table and sat across from each other.

The waiter approached and set two glasses of water on the table. "Hi, I'm Mason. I'll be your server this evening. May I start you off with something to drink?"

Simone shrugged. "I'm ready to order."

"Me too," Jabari said.

"Okay. What can I get for you, ma'am?" the waiter asked.

"I'll have the wings and gingerbread waffles with the maple pecan schmear and the calypso drizzle," Simone ordered.

"Any sides?" the waiter asked.

"Cheese grits and collard greens," she said, handing him the menu.

"Anything to drink?" the waiter asked.

"Sweet tea," she said.

"And you, sir?" the waiter asked.

"I'll have the classic waffles with drumsticks, with the strawberry cream schmear and the cashew caramel drizzle. I'll also have collard greens but with mac and cheese," he said.

"And to drink?" The waiter gazed at Jabari and squinted his eyes.

"Sweet tea," he said.

The waiter proceeded to the terminal and entered their orders. He later returned with two glasses of sweet tea and placed them on the table. "Your food will be right up," he said.

Jabari leaned back in his seat and surveyed the room. Several customers glanced at Jabari, and then averted their eyes.

"You sure you want to eat here?" Simone asked.

"Where can I go without being identified at this point?" Jabari said.

"How do you think this'll affect your work?"

"What do you mean?"

"Do you feel like you'll be able to do your job effectively once this blows over?" Simone sipped her tea.

Jabari let out a deep sigh. "I don't know."

"Will you stay on patrol?"

"I never planned to stay on patrol," he said.

"What do you see yourself doing in the next five years?"

"Make detective or work my way up to captain. The routine of patrol has worn thin, and I'm eager to move beyond it."

"I understand that," she said.

"I'm also working on expanding my real estate portfolio," he said.

"Rental properties?" she asked.

"I have a few apartment rentals. I could use a few more," he said.

The waiter returned with their food, placing their plates in front of them. "Enjoy."

Simone sprinkled a bit of hot sauce on her wings and set the bottle on the table.

"What about you?" Jabari asked.

"What?"

"Where do you see yourself in five years?"

"I don't know. It depends on where the best opportunities are. I'll stay at Central if I get tenure. Otherwise, I may go somewhere else to teach," she said.

"That's bullshit," a man yelled from the other side of the restaurant.

Cellular phones buzzed and rang throughout the restaurant.

"I knew they were gonna pull this shit," the man yelled, and then turned and glared at Jabari.

Jabari stared back until the man averted his eyes.

Simone reached for her phone and pulled up social media. She looked up at Jabari and said, "Not guilty."

Jabari slammed his fist on the table and lowered his head.

"How is he not guilty, Jabari?" Simone slumped back against the seat.

"How should I know," Jabari snapped.

Simone glared at him and furrowed her brow.

"I'm sorry," Jabari mumbled.

Simone's face softened. "It's okay." Her eyes shifted around the room.

"Do you want to pack this up to go?" he asked.

"No, I want to finish my food," she said.

The bartender changed the television to the local ABC News station, and all eyes shifted to the television.

Jabari and Simone remained at the table and quietly finished eating.

The waiter returned to the table and removed their empty plates. "Can I get you any dessert?" he asked.

"Peach cobbler," Simone said.

"Sweet potato pie," Jabari ordered.

"Coming right up," the waiter said, before stepping away.

Jabari eyed the paintings of Miles Davis and Satchmo hanging on the walls. The deceased musicians appeared to be staring at him. As sunlight faded outside, Jabari noticed an increase in the number of people on the streets. The waiter returned to the table with their desserts, his hands shaking as he placed their delicacies on the table.

Within an instant, Jabari noticed the number of people on the streets doubled. "I need to get you out of here."

Simone turned toward the window. "I'll be done in a minute," she said, defiantly.

The manager, a woman with curly gray hair, came to their table and stood next to the waiter. "Hey, listen. We're closing early."

"Okay, not a problem. I'll take the check," Jabari said.

"There's something you should know," the manager said.

"What's that?" Jabari asked.

The manager turned to the waiter. "Hey Mason, show him the tweet."

The waiter reached in his pocket and pulled out his phone. He opened Twitter and showed it to Jabari and Simone. The tweet was posted by the leader of the Justice League, and it was comprised of only five words. "Meet at Durham Central Park." The tweet had been shared more than fifteen hundred times in four minutes. The manager turned to the waiter and said, "Get their bill."

The waiter darted off toward the computer.

The manager turned back to their table and said, "Let me

clear everyone else out of here, and when the coast is clear, you can quietly slip out."

"Okay," Jabari agreed.

The restaurant staff settled all the customers' bills and cleared the restaurant.

Jabari handed the waiter his credit card and waited for him to return. Several staff members brought out posters that read, BLACK OWNED BUSINESS, and posted them in the windows, while two large men stood outside the door with their arms folded across their chests.

When the waiter returned with Jabari's credit card, Jabari signed the receipt and stood. "Let's go."

Simone took Jabari's hand as he guided her to the door.

Outside, Jabari saw swarms of protesters descending on the area from all directions, marching toward Durham Central Park, where Jabari had parked his truck. The city was dark and silent, and boots on pavement was the only sound he heard. Jabari and Simone fell in with the crowd, trying to blend in, hoping to make their way to the truck without incident.

As they passed the park, Jabari whispered to Simone, "Almost there."

"There's that pig," a man yelled.

"Shit." Jabari gripped Simone's hand and pulled her into the park where they lingered in the shadows near a brick wall. Jabari caught sight of a group, all donning black t-shirts emblazoned with the emblem of the Justice League in bold ivory font, as they made their entrance to the park, joining the multitude that had already convened. Congo drums thundered in the night.

A crowd stood around Mount Merrill with raised fists, where a young lady stood at a podium, reciting a heartfelt poem. Multiple protesters followed her and delivered heartfelt speeches and recited poems of protest.

Ultimately, the head of the Justice League made her way up Mount Merrill and grasped the microphone, and the crowd fell silent. Alongside her, fellow Justice League members positioned themselves, arms crossed.

"Who is that?" Simone asked.

"Raven Harris," he answered. "She's the one who sent the tweet, inviting everyone here," Jabari whispered. He turned his attention back to the woman, and watched her gaze sweep over the crowd, her eyes tinged with crimson sorrow.

With a solemn shake of her head, she began to speak, "Not in my city. Not in my city."

"Speak, sister," someone yelled.

"I look out at all of you tonight. Seeing so many faces who have been with me in this fight for far too long," she said.

"That's right."

"We've been to Staten Island, Minneapolis, Ferguson, D.C., Galveston, and Baton Rouge, but we never thought it would happen here. Not in the Bull City," she screamed into the microphone.

"Tell it like it is, sister!"

"But whenever we get too comfortable... Whenever we get too relaxed, they remind us who they are," she continued.

"That's right."

"Did you see it? Did you see what they did? We fought for five months to get that video released. It took protests, op-eds, podcasts, lawsuits, and we were stonewalled at every turn. We've been pulled over, harassed, arrested, our names dragged through the mud, all in the fight for justice," she said.

"Justice," the crowd screamed.

Jabari's heart raced within his chest, a relentless drumbeat, while he absorbed the words she spoke. He held Simone's hand, as he sought a chance to discreetly slip away, but caution held him back. Huddled against the wall, observing in the shadows, he continued to absorb her words, feeling a sense of vulnerability amid it all.

"And we see why they fought so hard. They didn't want us to know the truth. They didn't want us to see what they did. To see that they murdered that boy in cold blood," she screamed.

"Tell it."

"They thought we would forget. They thought we would walk away. But we will never forget what they did to our city. We will never forget Miles Goodwin. Say his name," she screamed.

"Miles Goodwin."

"Say his name."

"Miles Goodwin."

"Say his name."

"Miles Goodwin."

Their voices rang in Jabari's ears.

"We are gonna march to City Hall, and we'll make them feel our pain. We will make them feel what they did to us. No Justice, no Peace. Defund the Police," she screamed.

The crowd followed, *"No justice, no peace. Defund the police."*

"No justice, no peace, defund the police," she continued, before stepping down from Mount Merrill, and the crowd fell in behind her, as they marched toward City Hall, where the Durham Police Department was making its stand.

Chapter Sixteen

Hundreds of protesters filled Foster Street, from Durham Central Park to the old Durham Bulls Baseball Stadium.

"Say his name."

"Miles Goodwin."

"Say his name."

"Miles Goodwin," the crowd chanted, as they slowly marched through downtown Durham. The protesters seamlessly moved from one chant to another, before eventually settling on the one that represented their ultimate goal. "No justice, no peace. Defund the police. No justice, no peace. Defund the police."

Jabari held Simone's hand as they stealthily moved toward his truck, but the protesters were everywhere, and he didn't feel they could safely make it to the truck without being noticed. He stopped and looked around. "Your apartment is only a few blocks away. I think we can make it there on foot."

"Okay," she agreed.

They kept their heads low as they weaved through the sea

of protesters, and eventually, they turned on a side street and cut away from the crowds. They moved quickly across several blocks and turned onto North Mangum Street. They heard protesters chanting all around them.

A police van rode by and an officer inside shouted orders, "You are in violation of curfew. Clear the streets immediately."

Hand in hand, they continued toward Corcoran Street where a policeman stood blocking their path. "Turn around. You can't cross here."

"It's okay," Jabari said, and reached for his badge.

The officer gripped his firearm and yelled, "Stop."

"He's a cop, dammit," Simone screamed.

Jabari produced his badge and held it up.

The officer squinted his eyes and said, "Shit, Miller. I didn't realize that was you."

"It's all right," Jabari said.

"Is it?" Simone yelled.

"We're trying to get to her apartment on Corcoran Street," Jabari said.

"Come on through," the officer said.

Simone scowled at the officer as they passed him.

They looked toward City Hall and saw a wall of law enforcement officers and a spectacle of flashing lights. They arrived at Simone's building, and she punched in the security code and opened the door. They rushed inside and down a hallway to the elevator. They stepped inside and ascended to the 8th floor. They entered Simone's apartment and rushed to the window, peering down at the chaos below.

Simone opened a side-table drawer and pulled out a pair of black binoculars. She slid open the glass door leading out to the balcony. "Over here."

Jabari rushed onto the balcony and took in the turmoil churning below. He could see the protesters approaching from far off, singing and chanting along the way. As they turned the corner, headed for City Hall, the protesters were met by a line of officers dressed in riot gear, with shields and police dogs. Military-style vehicles blockaded the streets, and a helicopter circled overhead. It was an overwhelming show of force, an unprecedented sight within the City of Durham's history. The protesters appeared anxious, their postures tense as they stood motionless, conveying an air of uncertainty regarding their next steps.

A baritone voice started to sing, *"Do you FEEEEL like you've had it? And do you feel like going on? 'Cause I FEEEEL like I've had it. And I feel like keeping on. Do you FEEEEL like you've had it?"*

"Enough," hundreds of protesters shouted with raised fists.

Baritone: "Do you feel like going on?"

Protesters: "Enough! Enough!"

Baritone: "'Cause I FEEEEL like I've had it."

Protesters: "Enough!"

Baritone: "And I feel like keeping on."

Protesters: "Enough! Enough!"

Baritone: "Do you FEEEEL like you've had it?"

Protesters: "Enough!"

Baritone: "Do you feel like going on?

Protesters: "Enough! Enough!"

Baritone: "'Cause I FEEEEL like I've had it."

Protesters: "Enough!"

Baritone: "And I feel like keeping on."

"Enough! Enough!"

The protesters stood together swaying to the rhythm of the song. They eventually turned back toward the line of police and continued their march. They marched in rhythm toward the police, undeterred by the show of force. They moved with purpose toward whatever fate awaited them.

Baritone: "Because I FEEEEL like I've had it."

Protesters: "Enough!"

Baritone: "And I feel like keeping on."

Protesters: "Enough! Enough!"

Baritone: "Do you FEEEEL like you've had it?"

Protesters: "Enough!"

Baritone: "Do you feel like going on?"

Protesters: "Enough! Enough!" The protesters stopped in front of the police, marching in place, and singing loudly.

Baritone: "'Cause I FEEEEL like I've had it."

Protesters: "Enough!"

Baritone: "And I feel like keeping on."

Protesters: "Enough! Enough!"

Baritone: "Do you FEEEEL like you've had it?"

Protesters: "Enough!"

Baritone: "Do you feel like going on?"

Protesters: *"Enough! Enough,"* they sang, and stomped their feet in a rhythmic dance.

Airhorns sounded from multiple directions, and a man came forward, dancing between the officers and the protesters. Others joined him. They screamed their frustrations about the history of mistreatment toward their communities.

"I am not a threat to you. I am a man. I am a man," a protestor yelled.

A woman came forward holding a sign which read, "Stop Killing Us!" She shook the sign at the line of officers. They went on this way for a while, until the police had had enough.

"You are in violation of curfew. Clear the area," a sergeant ordered.

"We shall not be moved. We shall not be moved," the protesters chanted.

An ocean of protest signs waved in the air. The signs read, "Justice for Miles Goodwin" and "How Many Were Not

Filmed?" and "Miles' Life Mattered." Many protesters held photos of Miles Goodwin.

"This is your last warning. Clear the area now," the sergeant ordered.

"We shall not be moved. We shall not be moved!"

Several protesters stepped forward and took a knee.

"Squad, shields up," the sergeant ordered.

"Huhh," the officers grunted, as they raised their shields in front of their faces.

"Squad, gas up!"

"Huhh." A dozen officers pointed tear gas projectiles up toward the sky.

"Squad, fire!"

Mayhem ensued. Streams of tear gas fell from the sky. Rubber bullets and bean bags slammed into protesters from multiple directions. Riot batons shattered bones and lacerated skin as protesters scattered in multiple directions.

A line of police vehicles moved forward, pushing many protesters onto a side street where two military-style vehicles waited. Several officers appeared on rooftops, pointing their projectiles at the protesters. Streams of tear gas and rubber bullets were fired at the crowd, pushing them into a team of officers that charged the trapped protesters from behind the Humvees. The charging officers tackled men and women, restrained them with zip ties, and stuffed them into waiting vans. There was no escaping for the protesters.

Jabari stood on the balcony bewildered, as he peered down at the chaos. He saw the officers leaving the people with no avenue of escape—a clear violation of police policy and procedure. He knew that during crowd control tactics, police must always give protesters a path to withdraw. Jabari watched as bean bags and rubber bullets slammed into those surrounded.

A group of fleeing protesters forced a small opening in the

gate to a parking deck and crawled underneath. Others held up the gate for more to do the same, where they could run to the other side and escape into the night.

"What the fuck, Jabari?" Simone screamed at him with raised arms. "That's bullshit!"

Jabari turned to face her. "I know," he said.

"Well, do something," she yelled.

"What the fuck am I gonna do from here?" he yelled back.

"Call somebody, dammit!"

"Call who, Simone?"

She folded her arms and glared at him with tears burning her eyes. "You know what? I can't do this. I can't." She marched into her bedroom and slammed the door.

Jabari clenched his fists and yelled, "Fuck!"

Chapter Seventeen

The streets eventually cleared, and Jabari lay on Simone's couch trying to sleep, but he couldn't. On his back, he stared at the ceiling as his mind raced from one scene to another. He thought about all the chaos he had witnessed during his career and how he had escaped the fire a few days before. But forefront on his mind were scenes from the night of the shooting. Flashes of Miles Goodwin's bruised and bloody face and his frightened, shifty eyes. He saw the knife dropping from Miles' hand, and then the bullets tearing into his young chest. He thought of his testimony and wondered if he could have expressed himself any clearer.

The light of dawn eventually creeped into the living space. Jabari sat up and gazed out at the city. He picked up the phone and called Sergeant Cooper. He hadn't spoken to him since the night his brothers in blue stopped by to check on him.

"Hey, it's Miller," he said.

"Hey, Miller. Is everything all right?"

"I'm straight, but that was a real shitshow last night," Jabari said.

"The riot?" Sergeant Cooper asked.

"The ambush. What the fuck was that?"

"I wasn't a part of that. My crew was on traffic duty last night," Cooper assured him.

"It's not going to play well on the news," Jabari warned.

"Yeah, it probably won't," Cooper said.

"Y'all be safe out there tonight," Jabari said.

"Thanks, bro."

"Later." Jabari ended the call and immediately dialed his captain, but the call went to voicemail. He waited for the beep, then spoke clearly and firmly.

"Hi, Captain Lucas—this is Miller. I wanted to bring something important to your attention. I spent the night at a friend's place downtown, and from there, I had a clear view of the protest. What I saw was troubling. Officers were forcing protesters onto a side street, effectively trapping them with no avenue of escape. Then, from a rooftop position, they fired projectiles—ambushing them—and herded them into waiting paddy wagons.

"The tactic was a classic case of kettling, and if the media gets wind of it, there's going to be a serious backlash. I strongly recommend identifying who was responsible and making sure this doesn't happen again. You've got my number if you want to talk. Take care." With that, he ended the call.

Later, Jabari sat on Simone's couch, staring out at the horizon. He reached for the remote control and turned on the local news. The news showed Police Chief Justina Mathews standing outside of the Durham Police Department asking the community for calm. The news team went on to cover every angle of the protest. They interviewed citizens who supported the protesters and those who did not. Finally, the news switched to footage of the ambush, just as Jabari had predicted.

"Breaking news. Disturbing video shows Durham Police

kettling protesters onto a side street with no avenue of escape," the newsman announced.

The video showed peaceful protesters just before officers fired tear gas and rubber bullets from a nearby rooftop, while also dragging handcuffed protesters into nearby paddy wagons.

"Victoria Aiden is standing by with more," the newsman said.

"Yes, Anthony. I'm standing by with eyewitness, Yasmine Moreau, who was one of the protesters cornered here last night. Yasmine, please tell us what happened," Victoria Aiden said.

The young lady pushed braids away from her face and stared into the camera. *"My friends and I were standing down the street when the police started gassing us. We ran to escape the commotion and somehow ended up here. They blocked us in on both sides and we couldn't escape, and then they started gassing us and shooting at us. I was hit with something here."* She lifted her shorts, showing a blue and purple bruise on her thigh.

"How did you get away?" Victoria Aiden asked.

"Some guys lifted up that parking gate, and I crawled underneath it and ran to the other side," the young lady said, pointing.

"Motherfucker," Jabari said, stood and stomped to the window. Staring out at the city, he thought of his truck and wondered if it were still in one piece. He turned and looked toward Simone's bedroom door. It was still closed, sealing him out.

He sat on the sofa, pushed on his shoes and tied them. He stood and grabbed his wallet and keys and went to Simone's bedroom door. He placed a hand on the doorknob but didn't turn it. Instead, he pressed his ear to the door and listened. No TV and no social media—only silence. He remembered the last words she had said to him, "You know what, I can't do this. I can't," and the slamming of the door. *This is how it ends,* he thought. He shook his head and sighed. *We'll have this conversation later. I don't have it in me right now,* he thought.

He moped back into the kitchen and picked up a pen and a piece of paper. *Gone to get my truck. Talk later,* he wrote. He stepped out into the hallway and closed the door behind him. He rode the elevator down to the ground floor and stepped out onto the street.

Jabari surveyed the area. The streets were littered with trash and abandoned protest signs, but nothing appeared to be damaged, as far as he could tell. Crossing the street, he peered across at the bronze statue of Major the Bull, for a moment, he could've sworn the bull snorted at him, his breath bellowing out from his contorted nostrils. His path led him past the Carolina Theater, and alongside the Durham Chamber of Commerce building, where Miles Goodwin had taken his last breath. He continued to Durham Central Park, where Jabari found his truck sitting where they had left it.

Jabari surveyed the vehicle and let out a deep breath. *It seems to be in one piece,* he thought, before climbing inside. He started the engine and headed home. His phone rang and he saw Durham Police Department displayed across the touch screen. He tapped the screen and answered.

"Hi, Miller. It's Nia Nichols," the caller said.

"Hey, Nichols. What's going on?" he replied.

"It's a fucking madhouse around here," she said.

"I bet it is. What can I do for you?" he asked.

"The Chief wants to see you."

"She does? When?"

"Can you be here at ten?" she asked.

"I can do that."

"Good. See you soon," she said.

Jabari went straight home, hopped into the shower, and dressed in a pair of blue slacks, a gray dress shirt and a gray-

and-blue-striped tie. He slipped his feet into a pair of black Oxford shoes and headed to the station. He arrived and took the elevator up to the 4th floor.

"Hi, Nichols," Jabari said, when he saw Chief Mathews' assistant.

"Hey, Miller." Nia Nichols stepped from around the receptionist desk with open arms.

Jabari wrapped his arms around her and squeezed.

"One second." She then stepped to the chief's door and said, "Corporal Miller is here." She turned to Jabari and said, "Go on in."

Jabari stepped into the office. "Good morning, Chief Mathews."

"Corporal Miller," she said, rising to shake his hand. "Have a seat."

Jabari sat across from her and rested his hands on his lap.

"One hell of a night," she said.

"Yes, ma'am, it was."

"And it isn't over. We're expecting more protests tonight, and probably for several more days," she said.

"Yes, I expect the same," he replied.

Chief Mathews turned her gaze toward the window. The morning sun painted long streaks of gold across her desk.

"I heard you weren't pleased with how things were handled last night."

"No, ma'am. I wasn't." He kept his voice even. "It played right into the worst narratives about us."

She nodded slowly. "I agree. And I want you to know—the person behind that spectacle will be disciplined," she said.

"That's good to know," Jabari replied.

She leaned back in her chair, studying him. "We've been doing some quiet outreach. Taking the pulse of the community. People trust you, Corporal Miller."

"I appreciate that," Jabari said, careful not to sound too eager.

"That's why I called you here. We need you—are you ready to come back?" she asked.

He gave a single nod. "Yes, ma'am. I most certainly am," he said.

"Good." She smiled.

"You want me out on the streets tonight?" he asked.

"Oh, no. I don't think that would be the best use of your public image, Corporal. I need you to take on a more leadership role," she said.

"What do you have in mind?"

"I would like you to consider assuming the role of the Community Liaison Officer and Head of Professional Standards."

Jabari raised his eyebrows slightly. "What does that involve?"

"Your responsibilities would include cultivating connections with residents and community leaders. You will be the point of contact for addressing citizen inquiries pertaining to law enforcement matters, gathering insights from community members on police practices, and identifying community concerns. Your task will involve seeking resolutions that align with the perspectives of both the community and law enforcement.

Jabari looked out the window for a long moment before turning back to her. "The role sounds promising, but I have some reservations."

"Speak freely," came a reassuring response.

"With all due respect, I'm not inclined toward engaging in political maneuvers, nor do I wish to publicly endorse actions I disagree with. My interest would solely materialize if I'm afforded the independence and backing to facilitate substantial, meaningful changes," articulated Jabari.

"I understand your apprehension, and I want to assure you that this position won't be superficial. You'll report directly to Captain Lucas, and you'll provide weekly updates during command staff meetings. Additionally, as head of professional standards, you will take part in the incident review team and help inform necessary policy changes and training standards," she explained. "However, to commence..." Chief Mathews opened a desk drawer and pulled out a small velvet box, placing it on the desk in front of him.

When Jabari opened it, he found two silver sergeant pins inside.

"This role comes with a promotion," she said, gently.

Jabari turned the pins over in his hand. His chest tightened. For a moment, he couldn't speak, as a wave of emotions filled him.

"Are you interested?" she asked.

He looked up. "Yes, ma'am. Thank you for the opportunity."

"You've earned it. We'll have your pinning ceremony when things settle down." Chief Mathews rose, extending her hand. "Congratulations, Sergeant Miller."

Jabari stood and shook it firmly.

"I'll see you here first thing Monday morning," she announced.

"Yes, ma'am. Bright and early."

Jabari made his way downstairs and exited the building. He climbed into his truck and turned the key. His hand moved instinctively to his phone—he wanted to call Simone, to share his good news—but he hesitated. He stared at the screen for a moment, then dropped it on the console, shifted into gear, and pulled out onto East Main Street, heading home.

At home, he made himself an egg sandwich and brewed a cup of coffee. He carried the meal into the living room, turned on the television, and flipped through local news channels. Each network had their take on the protests, showing chaotic scenes from different angles—but he knew none truly captured what it felt like to be caught in the middle of it all. Eventually, he switched the TV off.

He busied himself around the house. First, by cleaning up the kitchen. He washed the dishes and put them away. He quickstepped into his home gym and stood facing his pull-up power station. He reached and grasped the bar above his head and did ten pull-ups. He stepped back into the kitchen and swept the floor before heading back to the gym for another set of ten pull-ups. He swept the living room floor before doing another ten pull-ups, and by the end of his tenth set, he had swept and vacuumed the entire house. Back in the gym, he loaded four 45-pound plates onto a barbell, totaling 225 pounds. He lay back on the bench and pressed weights from his chest ten times. He proceeded to complete ten sets of ten, resting two minutes between each set. He hadn't been in a public gym since the night of the shooting—making do with the little equipment he had at home. He was now ready to get back into the gym, where he could have a proper workout.

He drank a glass of water before heading to his bedroom closet to check on his uniforms. Two were pressed and still wrapped in plastic from the cleaners. "These'll get me through Tuesday," he muttered. He pulled three more from the closet, laid them across the bed, retrieved the ironing board, the iron, and a can of starch. One by one, he pressed the shirts and pants and hung them back neatly in the closet.

Jabari returned to the living room and stretched out on the couch. But the more he tried to relax, the more Simone occupied his thoughts. He shook her from his mind and moved into his home office and powered on his computer. He reviewed ledgers of his rental properties, scanned receipts, and organized digital folders.

He thought about his new position and what it would entail. He opened a file marked *Durham PD Policy and Procedures*, scrolling through it slowly, highlighting sections that would support him in his new role. When he'd exhausted every task he could think of, he made a cup of green tea, returned to the couch, and let the sounds of Luther Vandross and Keith Sweat fill the room. He lip-synced to Teddy Pendergrass, quietly mouthing, "I think I better let it go... looks like another love TKO," as the last rays of sunlight faded from the room.

Jabari had finally begun relaxing when he heard a knock. He stood, crossed the room, and opened the door to find Simone standing on the porch, fresh from the gym in yoga pants and a sports top. Her presence hit him all at once—a mix of relief and longing.

"Hey, Simone," he said, stepping aside.

"Hey." She stepped in, arms folded, eyes locked onto his. "Were you not going to call?"

"I picked up the phone, but..."

She squinted, unimpressed. "Red flag, Jabari," she said, wagging a finger.

Jabari sighed, "I just thought... you needed some space."

"No, what I need is to know where we stand," she said.

"I thought you were breaking it off," he said.

"We're adults. If I were breaking it off, I would've said so. Wait up, is that what you want? To break it off?" she asked.

"No."

"Then what do you want?"

He closed his eyes, rubbed the back of his neck. When he opened his eyes and met her gaze again, his voice was soft, "I want to never again feel like I've lost you."

Something in her expression shifted. Her posture softened, but her arms stayed folded. Jabari stepped closer, placed a hand gently on the small of her back, and pulled her in. He was relieved when she didn't resist. "I'm sorry." He pressed his lips against hers until he felt her arms loosen and wrap around his back.

She buried her face in his chest. "I'm sorry, too. I was just so angry."

"I know," he whispered. "You had every right."

They held each other tightly. "Oh, that reminds me. I have some news," he said.

"What kind of news?"

"I got a promotion."

Simone gave him a playful punch to the chest. "And you didn't *call* me?"

"I know. I'm sorry."

"Well? What's the title?"

Jabari took her hand and led her to the couch to sit.

"Okay already, tell me," she said.

He grinned. "Community Liaison Officer and Head of Professional Standards. You can call me that... or Sergeant Miller, if you're nasty."

"Oh, yes, Sergeant Miller, I love the sound of that." She laughed. "This requires a celebration." Simone stood, sauntered to the kitchen, uncorked a bottle of wine, and returned with two glasses. "Cheers, baby, I'm so happy for you."

Jabari smiled.

They brought their wine glasses together, "clink," and sipped the wine.

"So, what does the new role entail?" she asked, settling in beside him.

"Engaging the community, building trust between residents and police, and responding to public concerns. I'll also be part of the incident review team—helping update training standards and policies."

"Will you have the autonomy to make real changes?"

"I know what you're getting at, and the chief made it clear this isn't just for show. If it were, I wouldn't have taken it."

"Good, then you're the right man for the job."

He lay back on the couch and pulled her toward him. She brought her lips down to his, and the warmth of her tongue transported him to a higher plain. As the music played, they made up fully and passionately throughout the night, and they made up some more the next day.

Lying in bed, Simone studied his face. "Do you go to church?"

"Not regularly," he said. "I don't have a church home."

"You want to go?"

"Today?"

"If we leave in an hour, we'll make the eleven o'clock at White Rock."

He sighed. "Can we go next week?"

"We can. But after the week you've had... I think it'd be good for you."

"Next week. I promise."

"Okay," she said.

"What do you want to do today?"

"Just relax and prepare for tomorrow. It's been a hell of a week."

"I understand, but I'm gonna run home and get ready for church. I have a lot to be thankful for. "We barely escaped the fire with our lives. Sometimes I can still smell the smoke," she murmured, her voice far away. Then, more briskly, "Anyway, I'll be back later."

"Okay, the code to the front door and alarm is zero-four-two-one," he offered.

"Got it," she smiled.

Simone slipped out of bed, collected her clothes, and headed to the bathroom.

Jabari pulled on shorts and a t-shirt, then wandered into the living room. He sat on the couch and turned the TV to *Sports Center*.

Moments later, Simone sat beside him. "You hungry?" she asked.

"Starving."

She stood and sauntered to the kitchen and looked around. "Will you grab the oatmeal? I can't reach it," she called out.

Jabari stepped into the kitchen and pulled a container of steel-cut oats from the shelf. "Here you go."

"Thanks," she smiled. Simone diced apples, added them to boiling water with brown sugar and cinnamon, then stirred in steel-cut oats and turned the heat down. She ground fresh coffee and started the machine.

"Will you turn on the news?" she asked.

"Sure." Jabari sat on the couch and reached for the remote control.

After Simone brought Jabari a bowl of oatmeal and a cup of coffee, she returned to the kitchen and got her own and joined him on the couch. "Are they still at it?" she asked.

"They were last night, but the streets are clear now," he answered.

As they ate, a breaking news banner flashed across the screen, accompanied by Jabari's face.

"Durham Police Department names Jabari Miller as the new Community Liaison Officer and Head of Professional Standards," the anchor announced.

Simone grabbed the remote control and increased the volume.

"The role involves improving relationships with people who

live in the city of Durham, and informing police policy at the department. Police Chief Justina Mathews says they've learned a lot over the last year, and she wants the community to see the Durham Police Department improving and creating a better relationship between officers and community members that people can feel proud of. A press conference is scheduled for tomorrow to officially introduce him to the public."

Simone grinned. "Press conference?"

"She didn't mention one," Jabari said.

Simone squeezed his hand. "I'm so proud of you."

He smiled. "Thanks, baby."

"I need to head out," she said, glancing at the time.

They stepped out onto the driveway and headed to her car.

"How's it running?" he asked.

"Like new." She started the engine. "I'll be back after church."

He leaned in and kissed her. "Drive safe."

Simone waved as she pulled away.

Jabari stood in the driveway, watching until she disappeared down the street.

The End

Acknowledgments

First and foremost, I want to express my deepest gratitude to my wife, Karine, as well as my son, James, and daughter, Victoria for their unwavering support. I am also immensely proud of my nieces and nephews, whose encouragement means so much to me.

A heartfelt thank you to the early readers of *Bull City Blues* —Melanie "Missy" Ullah, and my daughter, Victoria—whose feedback and encouragement were invaluable in the early stages of this book.

I am deeply grateful to the editors at Before You Publish – Book Press for helping me bring my vision to life.

To Joe, Tenisha, Stephanie, and the Harris family—thank you for your steadfast friendship and support.

To the Chidley Hall First Floor Annex crew—Lemuel, Bernard, Jelani, Jossan, and Patrick—it's been a joy to watch you chase your dreams and achieve success. Thank you for being a constant source of inspiration.

Finally, I want to extend my appreciation to the brothers of Gamma Beta and my NCCU family for their constant encouragement and support.

About the Author

After many years in both law enforcement and corrections, **Wynton Sellers** gained valuable insight into the complex and often tense relationship between law enforcement and the communities they serve. *Bull City Blues* was inspired by the many police-involved shootings that have taken place across the United States, some justified, others deeply controversial. Through this work, Sellers explores the critical moment when an officer must decide whether to use lethal force.

Wynton Sellers lives in North Carolina with his wife and children.

Also by Wynton Sellers

Grandfather Mountain

Alexander Merchant is flourishing in the social world of Needham Broughton High when he meets Natalie Agadani and falls in love. Alexander and Natalie are swept into a whirlwind teenage romance, but when Alexander unwittingly commits a crime, Natalie, who could be the love of his life, is sent away, leaving him to face the fallout of their indiscretions alone. In prison, Alexander must learn to navigate the social constructs of the inmate world, a cesspool of desperation, violence, and despair, where one wrong decision could determine life and death. Can Alexander make it out unscathed? Or will the system change him forever?

9 798999 323491 5